because I'm worth it

a gossip girl
novel

because I'm worth it
a gossip girl novel

by
Cecily von Ziegesar

LITTLE, BROWN AND COMPANY

New York 〜 Boston

Little, Brown and Company
Time Warner Book Group
1271 Avenue of the Americas, New York, NY 10020
Visit our Web site at www.lb-teens.com

First Edition

 Produced by 17th Street Productions,
an Alloy company
151 West 26th Street, New York, NY 10001

ISBN 0-316-90968-8

10 9 8 7 6 5 4 3
CWO
Printed in the United States of America

It makes one feel rather good deciding not to be a bitch. . . .
—Ernest Hemingway
The Sun Also Rises

Disclaimer: All the real names of places, people, and events have been altered or abbreviated to protect the innocent. Namely, me.

hey people!

February is like the girl at that party I threw when my parents took a "second honeymoon" in Cabo last week (I know: sad). You remember—the girl who puked all over the Spanish marble floor in the guest bathroom and then refused to leave? We had to throw her Dior saddlebag and Oscar de la Renta embroidered sheepskin coat into the elevator before she finally got the message. Unlike most places in the world, though, New York refuses to fall into a February-induced depression and become a cold, gray, dismal wasteland. At least, *my* New York does. Here on the Upper East Side we all know the cure for the drearies: one of Jedediah Angel's crazy-sexy party dresses, a pair of black satin Manolos, that new "Ready or Not" red lipstick you can only get at Bendel's, a good Brazilian bikini wax, and a generous slathering of Estée Lauder self-tanner, in case your St. Barts tan left over from Christmas break has finally faded. Most of us are second-semester seniors—*at last*. Our college applications are in and our schedules are light, with a double free period every day during which we can catch a Fashion Week runway show or head back to a friend's penthouse apartment to drink skinny lattes, smoke cigarettes, and help pick out the evening's screw-homework party outfit.

Another redeeming thing about February is my all-time favorite should-be-a-national-no-school-holiday, Valentine's Day. If you already have a sweetheart, lucky you. If you don't, now's the chance to put the moves on that hottie you've been drooling over all winter. Who knows? You might find true love, or at least true lust, and soon *every* day will feel like Valentine's Day. Either that or you can just sit at home IMing sad, anonymous notes to people and eating heart-shaped chocolates until you can't fit into your favorite pair of Seven jeans anymore. It's up to you. . . .

Sightings

S and **A** holding hands and wandering slowly down **Fifth Avenue** to the bar at the **Compton Hotel**, where they can be seen most Friday nights, quaffing **Red Bull** and **Veuve Clicquot** cocktails and chuckling to themselves with the heady knowledge that they are without a doubt the hottest couple in the room. **B** refusing to go inside **Veronique**—a maternity store on Madison—with her glowingly pregnant mom. **D** and **V** wearing matching black turtlenecks, their legs intertwined as they watched that twisted, depressing **Ken Mogul** film downtown at the **Angelika.** They're two morbid, artistic, weirdo peas in a pod—so insanely perfect for each other, you want to shout at them, "Hey, what took you so *long*?!" **J** on the Ninety-sixth Street crosstown bus, carefully studying a billboard for breast-reduction surgery. I'd definitely go for it if I were in her double-D cups . . . um, I mean shoes. The ever-adorable **N** playing a stoned game of ice-hockey golf with his buddies at **Sky Rink.** He doesn't seem to mind being girlfriendless. It's not like he'll have any trouble finding a new one. . . .

And finally: *Who's getting in early??*

This week an annoying little group of us is going to find out whether or not we got early admission to the top colleges in the country. This is it. There's no more time for our parents to build another new wing on the library. No time to bribe another esteemed alum into sending the dean of admissions a letter of recommendation. No time to star in another school play. The envelopes are already in the mail.

I'd like to take a moment to point out that the decision is completely arbitrary because basically we're all perfect specimens. We're gorgeous, intelligent, well mannered and eloquent, with influential parents and perfect transcripts (except for the occasional blip, like getting kicked out of boarding school or having to take the SATs eight times).

I'd also like to give a word of advice to those of us who *do* get in early: Try not to talk about it *too* much, okay? The rest of us have a couple more months of waiting to do, and if you want to get invited out with us, you'd better not even mention the words *Ivy League* in our presence. Our parents do that quite enough already, thank you very much. Not that it's a sore subject or anything.

I think it's safe to say we're all suffering from late-winter waiting-to-hear-from-colleges cabin fever. It's time to run a little wild! Just think, the later we stay out, the quicker the days will blur by. And believe me, every wicked thing we get up to will be glamorized, dissected, and blown totally out of proportion right here by yours truly. Have I ever let you down?

You know you love me.

gossip girl

b bonds with *j* over breast size

"Just a few fries and some ketchup, please," Jenny Humphrey told Irene, the one-hundred-year-old bearded lunch lady behind the counter in the basement cafeteria of the Constance Billard School for Girls. "Just a *few*," Jenny repeated. Today was the first day of peer group, and Jenny didn't want her senior peer group leaders to think she was a total pig.

Peer group was a new program the school was trying out. Every Monday at lunchtime the freshman girls were to meet in groups of five with two senior girls to discuss peer pressure, body image, boys, sex, drugs, alcohol, and any other issues that might be bothering the freshman girls or that the two senior peer group leaders deemed important enough to talk about. The idea was that if the older girls shared their experiences with the younger girls and started a sympathetic dialogue, the younger girls would make informed decisions instead of stupid high-school-career-damaging mistakes that might embarrass their parents or the school.

With its beamed ceiling, mirrored walls, and birchwood modernist tables and chairs, the Constance Billard School cafeteria looked more like a hot new restaurant than an institutional dining room. The dingy old cafeteria had been redone last summer because so many students had been going out for lunch or bringing their own that the school had been losing money on wasted food. The new cafeteria had won an architectural prize for its appealing design and high-tech kitchen, and it was now the students' favorite in-school hangout, despite the fact that Irene and her mean, stingy, grubby-fingernailed old cronies were still the ones serving the food from the cafeteria's updated, nouvelle American menu.

Jenny wove her way through the clusters of girls in pleated navy blue, gray, or maroon wool uniform skirts, picking at their wasabi-smoked tuna burgers and Red Bliss pommes frites and chatting about the parties they'd been to this past weekend. She slid her stainless steel tray onto the empty round table that had been reserved for peer group A and sat down with her back to the mirrored wall so she wouldn't have to look at herself while she ate. She couldn't wait to find out who her senior peer group leaders were going to be. Supposedly the competition had been fierce, since being a leader was a relatively painless way of showing colleges that you were still involved in school activities even though your applications were already in. It was like getting extra credit for eating fries and talking about sex for fifty minutes.

Who wouldn't want to do that?

"Hello, Ginny." Blair Waldorf, the bitchiest, vainest girl in the entire senior class, or maybe the entire world, slid her tray into the place across from Jenny and sat down. She tucked a wavy lock of dark brown shoulder-length hair behind her ear and muttered at her reflection in the wall of mirrors. "I can't wait for my haircut." She glanced at Jenny, picked up her fork, and raked it through the dollop of whipped cream on top of her chocolate angel food cake. "I'm one of the leaders for peer group A. Are *you* in group A?"

Jenny nodded, clutching the seat of her chair as she stared gloomily down at her plate of cold, greasy fries. She couldn't believe her bad luck. Not only was Blair Waldorf the most intimidating senior in the school, she was also Nate Archibald's ex-girlfriend. Blair and Nate had always been the perfect couple; the ones destined to stay together forever and ever. Then, strange as it might have seemed, Nate had actually dumped Blair for Jenny after meeting Jenny in the park and sharing a joint with her.

It had been Jenny's first joint, and Nate had been her first love. She'd never dreamed of having an older boyfriend, let alone one as gorgeous and cool as Nate. But after a couple of too-good-to-be-true months, Nate had gotten bored with Jenny and had proceeded to break her heart in the cruelest way by ditching her on New Year's Eve. So now she and Blair Waldorf actually had something in common—they'd both been dumped by the same boy. Not that that made any difference. Jenny was pretty sure that Blair still hated her guts.

Blair knew perfectly well that Jenny was the balloon-boobed freshman whore who'd stolen her Natie away, but she also knew that Nate had dumped Jenny flat on her ass after some extremely embarrassing pictures of Jenny's bare butt in a thong had been posted on the Web just before New Year's Eve. Blair figured Jenny had already gotten her comeuppance, and she really couldn't be bothered with hating her anymore.

Jenny looked up. "Who's your coleader?" she asked timidly. She wished the other members of the group would hurry up and get there before Blair tore her head off with her perfectly manicured opalescent-pink fingernails.

"Serena's coming." Blair rolled her eyes. "You know her. She's always late." She combed her fingers through her hair, envisioning the cut she was going to get when she went for her appointment during double free period. She was going to have them do a mahogany rinse to get rid of the copper-colored highlights, and then she wanted it cut short, in a modern, superstylish sort of way, like Audrey Hepburn in *How to Steal a Million*.

"Oh," Jenny replied, relieved. Serena van der Woodsen was Blair's best friend, but she wasn't nearly as intimidating, because she was actually *nice*.

"Hi, guys. Is this peer group A?" A gangly, freckled freshman girl named Elise Wells sat down next to Jenny. She smelled like baby powder, and her strawlike blond hair was cut in a chin-length bob with thick bangs masking her forehead, exactly like the haircut Nanny gave you when you were two. "I'm just going to tell you now that I have a problem with eating," Elise announced. "I can't eat in public."

Blair nodded and pushed her slice of chocolate cake away from her. In peer group leader training the health teacher, Ms. Doherty, had told them to *listen* and try to be *sensitive*, putting themselves in the younger girls' shoes. Ms. Doherty should talk. All she ever talked about in ninth-grade health class was the boyfriends she'd had and all the sexual positions she'd tried. Still, Ms. Doherty was one of the teachers Blair had hit up for an extra recommendation to send to the Yale admissions office, and she really wanted to stand out as the best peer group leader in the senior class. She wanted her peer group freshmen to like her—no, *adore* her—and if one of them had a problem with eating in public, Blair wasn't going to sit there gorging herself on chocolate cake, especially not when she'd been planning to throw it up as soon as the bell rang anyway.

Blair pulled a pile of handouts out of her red Louis Vuitton bowling bag. "Body image and self-esteem are two of the issues we'll be discussing today," she told Elise and

Jenny, trying to sound professional. "If my coleader and the rest of our group ever decide to get here," she added impatiently. Was it physically possible for Serena to *ever* be on time?

Apparently not.

Just then, in a flurry of dove-gray cashmere and shimmering pale blond hair, Serena van der Woodsen slid her shapely, tanned butt into the chair next to Blair. The three other peer group A freshman girls were trailing her like baby ducklings. "Look what we suckered Irene into giving us!" Serena crowed, slapping a heaping plate full of greasy onion rings down in the middle of the table. "I told her we were having a special meeting and we were *starving*."

Blair glanced sympathetically at Elise, who was glowering at the plate of onion rings with blond-lashed blue eyes that would have been pretty if she'd tried using a little dark brown Stila lengthening mascara. "You're late," Blair accused, passing out the handouts to Serena and the other three freshmen. "I'm Blair," she told them. "And you are . . . ?"

"Mary Goldberg, Vicky Reinerson, and Cassie Inwirth," the three girls responded in unison.

Elise nudged Jenny's elbow. Mary, Vicky, and Cassie were the most annoyingly inseparable threesome in the freshman class. They were always brushing each other's hair in the hallways, and they did everything together, including pee.

Blair glanced down at the handout and read aloud, "Body image: accepting and embracing who you are." She looked up and smiled at the freshmen expectantly. "Do any of you have a particular body image issue you'd like to talk about?"

Jenny felt the blood creep into her neck and face as she boldly considered telling them about the breast-reduction consultation. But before she could get the words out, Serena crammed an enormous onion ring into her delicate mouth and interjected, "Can I just say something first?"

Blair frowned at her best friend, but Mary, Vicky, and Cassie were nodding eagerly. Listening to anything Serena van der Woodsen had to say was so much more interesting than any stupid body image discussion.

Serena plunked her elbows down on top of the handout and rested her perfectly chiseled chin in her manicured hands, her enormous dark blue eyes gazing dreamily at her idyllic reflection in the mirrored wall. "I'm so in love," she sighed.

Blair clutched her fork and dug into the piece of chocolate cake again, forgetting about her no-eating solidarity with Elise. Serena was so goddamned insensitive. First of all, the guy she was apparently "so in love" with happened to be Blair's new pseudohippie, guitar-playing, dreadlocked step-brother, Aaron Rose, which was just *so absurd*. And second of all, even though Nate had dumped Blair way back in November, Blair was *still* not over Nate, and the mere mention of the world *love* made her want to blow chunks. "I think we're supposed to get *them* to talk about *their* problems, not talk about *ourselves*," she hissed at Serena. Of course, if Serena had actually bothered to show up for peer group training, she would have known that herself.

Serena had blown the training off so she could go to a movie with Aaron, and, like a gullible idiot, Blair had covered for her. She'd told Ms. Doherty that Serena had a migraine but that she would personally go over all the major points they covered in training when Serena felt better. It was so typical. Whenever Blair did anything nice for someone else, she usually regretted it.

Which kind of explained why she was such a bitch most of the time.

Serena shrugged her halter-top-perfect shoulders. "I think love is a much better topic than body image anyway. I mean, we all talked body image to death in ninth-grade health." She glanced at the freshmen seated around the table. "Right?"

"I just think we should follow the handout," Blair insisted stubbornly.

"It's up to you guys," Serena told the younger girls.

Mary, Vicky, and Cassie waited, ears pricked, for the scoop on Serena's love life. Elise reached out and poked a greasy onion ring with a trembling, chewed-on fingernail and then snatched her hand away again as if she'd been burned. Jenny licked her winter-chapped lips. "Since we're supposed to talk about body image, I guess I have something to say," she told the group, her voice wavering. She looked up to find Blair nodding and smiling at her encouragingly.

"Yes, Ginny?"

Jenny looked down at the table again. Why was she even telling them this? *Because I need to tell someone,* she realized. She forced herself to keep talking despite the furious red-hot blush of embarrassment burning her face. "This weekend I almost had a consultation for a breast reduction."

Mary, Vicky, and Cassie scooted forward in their chairs to listen. Not only was peer group going to be *the* place to pick up the latest fashion trends from the two coolest girls in school, it was going to be a major resource for gossip!

"I made the appointment," Jenny continued, "but then I didn't go." She pushed her plate away and took a sip of water, trying to ignore the curious stares of the other girls. The group was riveted, and stealing the spotlight from Blair and Serena was no easy feat.

Elise picked up an onion ring, took a tiny bite, and

dropped it on the plate again. "What made you change your mind?" she asked.

"You don't have to answer that," Blair interrupted, remembering something Ms. Doherty had said in their training session about not pushing the members of the group to open up before they were ready. She glanced at her coleader. Serena was busy examining her split ends with a dreamy, faraway look, as if she hadn't heard a word anyone had said. Blair turned back to Jenny and tried to think of something reassuring to say so Jenny wouldn't feel like she was the only one in the group with breast-size issues.

"I always wanted bigger breasts. I've seriously considered getting implants." It wasn't a total lie. She was only a B cup and had always aspired to a C.

Who hasn't?

"Really?" Serena demanded, drifting back to earth. "Since when?"

Blair took another angry bite of cake. Was Serena purposely trying to sabotage her leadership skills? "You don't know everything about me," she snapped.

Cassie, Vicky, and Mary kicked each other under the table. This was so exciting! Serena van der Woodsen and Blair Waldorf were having a fight, and they were witnessing every word of it!

Elise combed her chewed-on fingernails through her thick blond bob. "I think it was really, um, amazing of you to tell us about that, Jenny." She smiled shyly at Jenny. "And I think it was brave of you not to do it."

Blair scowled. Why hadn't *she* said something about how brave Jenny was instead of making that outrageous statement about wanting implants? Who knew what these stupid freshmen were going to say about her once the group broke up?

Then she remembered something else Ms. Doherty had gone over in their training session.

"Oops. I think we were supposed to say something about confidentiality before we started. You know, like, nothing we say here will be repeated outside the group, or whatever?"

Too late. In a matter of minutes every girl in the school would be discussing Blair Waldorf's upcoming breast-implant job. *I heard she's waiting until the day after graduation* . . . etc., etc.

Jenny shrugged. "It's okay. I don't care who you tell." It wasn't like she could hide her enormous boobs anyway. They were just *there*.

Elise bent down and picked up her beige Kenneth Cole backpack. "Um, there are only eight minutes left before the bell rings. Is it all right if I go out and buy a yogurt now?" she asked.

Serena nudged the plate of onion rings towards Elise. "Have some more of these," she offered generously.

Elise shook her head, her freckled face flushed pink. "No, thanks. I don't eat in public."

Serena frowned. "Really? That's weird." She winced as Blair elbowed her in the arm, *hard*. "Ow! God, what was that for?"

"Maybe if you'd actually gone to peer group leader training, you'd get it," Blair growled under her breath.

"Can I go now?" Elise asked again.

It occurred to Blair that the peer group freshmen would really love her if she let them all go early. She could use the extra eight minutes to get to the hair salon on time anyway. "You can *all* go," she said, smiling sweetly, "unless you really want to stay and listen to Serena talk about *love* for the rest of the period."

Serena stretched her arms over her head and grinned up at the ceiling. "I could talk about love all day."

Jenny stood up. Ever since Nate had ditched her, love was the last thing she wanted to talk about. Funny—she'd thought Blair was going to be the peer group leader she couldn't deal with, but it was turning out to be Serena.

Elise stood up, too, tugging on her oversized pink turtleneck sweater as if it was too tight. "No offense, but if I don't eat a yogurt before lunch is over, I'm going to pass out in geometry."

"I'll come buy one with you," Jenny told her, using that as an excuse to leave the table.

"I may as well walk out with you guys," Blair yawned, standing up, too.

"Where are you going?" Serena demanded innocently. Normally on Mondays after lunch the two girls spent their luxurious double free period at Jackson Hole, drinking cappuccinos and making wild and fabulous plans for the summer after graduation.

"None of your business," Blair snapped. She'd been going to invite Serena to come with her to the salon, but now that Serena was being such a self-involved princess bitch, that was totally out of the question. She flipped her hair over her shoulder and slung her bag over her arm. "See you guys next week," she added to Mary, Vicky, and Cassie as she followed Jenny and Elise through the exit and up the back stairs to Ninety-third Street.

Back in the crowded cafeteria, Vicky leaned forward across the half-empty table. "So, *tell* us," she urged Serena.

Mary took a sip of one-percent milk and nodded eagerly. "Yes, yes. *Tell*."

Cassie tightened her light brown ponytail. "Tell us *everything*."

a very different kind of homework

"So what do you want to film first?" Daniel Humphrey asked his best friend and girlfriend of six weeks, Vanessa Abrams. Dan attended renowned Upper West Side boys school Riverside Prep, while Vanessa attended Constance Billard, but they had gotten permission to collaborate on a special senior project called *Making Poetry*. Vanessa, a budding film director, was going to film Dan, a budding poet and occasional star of Vanessa's films, writing and revising his poems.

Not exactly box-office-smash material, but Dan was so cute in a scruffy, rumpled, angst-ridden-artist sort of way that people would probably want to see it anyway.

"Just sit down at your desk and write something in one of those black notebooks like you always do," Vanessa instructed, peering through the lens of her digital video camera to see if the light was okay. "Can you clear some of that shit off your desk?"

Dan swept his arm over the desk and sent pens, paper clips, scraps of paper, rubber bands, books, empty packs of unfiltered Camels, matchbooks, and empty Coke cans crashing to the brown-carpeted floor. They were filming in Dan's room because that was where he usually worked. Besides, it was a straight shot through the park from Constance Billard on East Ninety-third Street between Fifth and Madison to Dan's apartment building on West Ninety-ninth Street and West End Avenue.

"And maybe take your shirt off, too," Vanessa suggested. *Making Poetry* was going to be about the artistic process, illustrating that what *doesn't* go into the work is just as important as what does. There would be lots of shots of Dan crumpling up paper and throwing it angrily across the room. Vanessa wanted to show that writing—or creating anything, for that matter—wasn't just a mental exercise: it was *physical*. Plus, Dan had these great little muscles in his back that she couldn't wait to get on film.

Dan stood up and peeled off his plain black T-shirt, tossing it onto his unmade bed where the Humphreys' fat old cat, Marx, lay asleep on his back like a furry beached whale. Everything about the apartment Dan shared with his father, Rufus, an editor of lesser-known Beat poets, and his little sister, Jenny, was unmade, falling apart, or at the very least completely covered with cat hair and dust bunnies. It was a large, bright, high-ceilinged apartment, but it hadn't been properly cleaned in twenty years, and the crumbling walls were gasping for a new coat of paint. Dan and his father and sister rarely threw anything away, either, so the sagging furniture and scratched wooden floors were strewn with old newspapers and magazines, out-of-print books, incomplete decks of cards, used batteries, and unsharpened pencils. It was the kind of place where your coffee got cat hair in it the minute you poured it, which was a problem Dan dealt with constantly because he was completely addicted to caffeine.

"Do you want me to face the camera?" he asked, sitting down on his worn wooden desk chair and swiveling it toward

Vanessa. "I could hold the notebook in my lap and write like this," he demonstrated.

Vanessa knelt down and squinted through the camera lens. She was wearing her gray pleated Constance Billard uniform with black tights, and the brown shag carpet felt bristly against her knees. "Yes, that's nice," she murmured. Oh, just look how pale and smooth Dan's chest was! She could see every rib, and that nice line of tawny peach fuzz that ran up his belly to his navel! She inched forward on her knees, trying to get as close as possible without ruining the frame.

Dan bit the end of his pen, smiled to himself, and then wrote, *She's got a shaved head, she wears black all the time, she needs a new pair of combat boots, and she hates to wear makeup. But she's the kind of girl who believes in you and secretly gets your best poem published in* The New Yorker. *I guess you could say I love her.*

It was probably the corniest thing he'd ever written, but it wasn't like he was going to publish it in his "Greatest Works" or anything.

Vanessa inched forward some more, trying to capture the fervent white of Dan's knuckles as he scribbled away. "What are you writing?" She pressed the record-sound button on her camera.

Dan looked up, grinning at her through his messy bangs, his golden brown eyes shining. "It's not a poem. It's just a little story about you."

Vanessa felt her whole body warm up. "Read it out loud."

Dan scratched his chin self-consciously and then cleared his throat. "Okay. 'She's got a shaved head . . . ,'" he began, reading what he'd written.

Vanessa blushed as she listened and then dropped the camera on the floor. She walked on her knees over to where

Dan was sitting, pushed his notebook out of the way, and laid her head in his lap.

"You know how we're always talking about having sex but we've never done it?" she whispered, her lips brushing the rough cloth of his army-green cargo pants. "Why don't we do it right now?"

Beneath her cheek she felt Dan's thigh muscle tighten. "Now?" He looked down and traced his finger along the edge of Vanessa's ear. She had four piercings in each ear, but none of them had earrings in them. He took a deep breath. He'd been saving sex for a moment when it seemed poetic and *right*. Maybe that time was *right now*, a spontaneous moment. It seemed especially apt and ironic when in exactly an hour he'd be back at Riverside Prep, sitting in last-period AP Latin, listening to Dr. Werd read Ovid in his over-the-top Latin-nerd accent.

Introducing double-free-period sex—the latest offering on the spring curriculum.

"Okay," Dan agreed. "Let's do it."

gossipgirl.net

topics ◄ *previous*   *next* ►   *post a question*   *reply*

Disclaimer: All the real names of places, people, and events have been altered or abbreviated to protect the innocent. Namely, me.

hey people!

Early rejection

So I heard the Ivies have come up with a conspiracy to maintain their intrigue and exclusivity: This year they're not accepting *anyone* early. Maybe it's only a false rumor. But if you don't get in early, try to think of it this way: Maybe you were *too* perfect. They just couldn't handle it. And just think how much fun we'll have if we all wind up at the same community college!

To surgically enhance or not, that is the question

The idea of surgically altering one's body in any way has always freaked me out, not because I don't think Dolly Parton looks great. She doesn't look a day over forty and she must be two hundred by now. But I'd be worried the doctors would make a mistake and deflate one breast entirely or leave out a nostril or something. Of course I'm as girly a girl as girls come, and I know how important it is to feel good about my appearance. I try to think of it this way though: You know when you see a gorgeous boy on the street and you say to your friend, "Look at *him*!" and then your friend makes a face like, *ugly*? We all have such *totally* varied tastes that someone is going to look at you and think, *yum-yum* dee-*lish*, no matter what *you* think you look like. You just have to learn to see what they see.

Your e-mail

Q: Dear G-Girl,
I heard you got in early to Bryn Mawr and you're psyched

because you like going to school with girls and you're this huge volleyball-playing lesbo. Tee hee.
—dorf

 Hello dorf,
What kind of a name is dorf, anyway? I refuse to stoop to your level of humor or tell you where I applied to college, but my mother and sister both happened to go to Bryn Mawr, and guess what? They're both *hot*.
—GG

Gotta dash home and check the mail for an important-looking business-sized envelope that may or may not dotormine my entire near future. Wish me luck!

You know you love me.

gossip girl

waspoid prince tries to score

When last-period French was finally over, Nate Archibald bid a hasty *à demain* to his St. Jude's School classmates and hurried up Madison Avenue to the pizza place on the corner of Eighty-sixth Street, the workplace of his dependable pot dealer, Mitchell. Lucky for Nate, St. Jude's was the oldest boys' school in Manhattan and had kept its tradition of ending the school day at 2 P.M. for both lower- and upper-school boys, even though most of the other city schools let out at 4 P.M. The school's reasoning was that it gave the boys extra time to play sports and do the copious amounts of homework they were sent home with every afternoon. It also gave them plenty of time to kick back and get high before, during, and *after* they played sports and did their homework.

The last time Nate had seen Mitchell, the wisecracking Kangol hat–wearing dealer had said he'd be moving back home to Amsterdam very soon. Today was Nate's last chance to score the biggest bag of sweet, Peruvian-grown weed Mitchell could provide. Blair had always complained about Nate's pot-smoking when they were together, whining about how boring it was to watch him staring at the Persian rug on her bedroom floor for ten minutes when they could have been fooling around or at a party somewhere. Nate had always maintained that his pot-smoking was a mere indulgence, like eating chocolate—something he could give up any time. And just to prove it—not that he *needed* to prove anything to Blair anymore—he was going to go cold turkey after he'd smoked every last leaf of pot from the giant bag he was going to buy today. If he were careful, he could make the bag last a good eight weeks. Until then he preferred not to even *think* about quitting.

"Two plain slices," Nate told the gangly, balding pizza chef wearing a bright purple WELCOME TO LOSERVILLE T-shirt. He rested his elbows on the pizza joint's red linoleum countertop, nudging aside plastic containers filled with garlic salt, red pepper flakes, and oregano. "Where's Mitchell?"

Mitchell's little side business was no secret in the pizza parlor. The pizza chef raised his bushy black eyebrows. His name might actually have been Ray, but even after years of buying pizza and pot there Nate still wasn't sure. "Mitchell's gone already. You missed him."

Nate patted the back pocket of his khakis, where he'd shoved his bulging Coach wallet, a sour lump of panic rising in his throat. Of course he wasn't *addicted*, but he didn't like being stuck without any weed at all when he'd been planning to roll a nice big fatty to while away the afternoon. And tomorrow afternoon, and the day after that . . .

"What? You mean he left for Amsterdam already?"

Ray—or maybe it was Roy—pulled open the shiny chrome door of the pizza oven and in one expert motion slipped two hot slices onto a double layer of paper plates and slid them across the counter in Nate's direction. "Sorry, buddy," he said only half sympathetically. "But from now on we sell pizza and soda and *only* pizza and soda. Got it?"

Nate picked up the plate of pizza and then put it down on the counter again. He couldn't believe his bad luck. He pulled out his wallet and removed a ten-dollar bill from the fat wad inside. "Keep the change," he muttered, dropping the bill on the counter before leaving with his pizza.

Out on the street, he wandered aimlessly toward the park, feeling like an abandoned dog. He'd been buying weed from Mitchell ever since eighth grade. One random May afternoon, Nate and his buddy Jeremy Scott Tompkinson had gone into the pizza place to buy a slice, and Mitchell had overheard Jeremy daring Nate to steal the container of oregano so they could take it home and smoke it. Mitchell had proposed to sell them something even more mood-enhancing, and Nate and his buddies had been coming back ever since. What was he supposed to do now, buy dime bags from one of those random, shifty-looking dudes in Central Park? Most of those guys sold crappy, dry, Texas-grown stuff anyway, not the succulent green buds Mitchell got directly from his uncle in Peru. Besides, he'd heard half the Central Park dealers were narcs just waiting to bust a kid like him.

Dumping his half-eaten pizza slices in the nearest garbage can, Nate dug into the pockets of his Hugo Boss naval officer–style coat, searching for a leftover roach. When he found one he crossed Fifth Avenue and crouched on a park bench to light it, ignoring the group of giggling tenth-grade girls in dark blue Constance Billard uniforms ogling him lustily as they walked by.

With his I-know-I'm-hot smile, his golden brown hair, his emerald green eyes, his always-tanned skin, and his sexy expertise in building and racing sailboats, Nate Archibald was the most lusted-after boy on the Upper East Side. He didn't have to go looking for girls. They just fell into his lap. Literally.

Nate sucked hard on the burning roach and pulled his cell

phone out of his pocket. The problem was, his other stoner St. Jude's buddies—Jeremy Scott Tompkinson, Charlie Dern, and Anthony Avuldsen—all bought from Mitchell, too. Mitchell was the best. But it was worth calling just to find out if any of them had managed to score a big stash before their dealer had disappeared.

Jeremy was in a cab on his way to an interschool squash club game at the Ninety-second Street Y. "Sorry, dude," his voice crackled over the line. "I've been doing mom's Zoloft all day. Why don't you just buy a dime bag from one of those dealers in the park or something?"

Nate shrugged. Something about buying a dime bag in the park seemed so . . . *lame*. "Whatever, man," he told Jeremy. "See you tomorrow."

Charlie was in the Virgin megastore, buying DVDs with his little brother. "Bummer," he said when Nate told him about the situation. "But you're right near the park, right? Just buy a dime bag."

"Yeah, whatever," Nate replied. "See you tomorrow."

Anthony was having a driving lesson in the new BMW M3 sports car his parents had given him for his eighteenth birthday last weekend. "Check your mom's medicine cabinet," he advised. "Parents are the ultimate resource."

"I'll look into it," Nate answered. "Later." He clicked off and sucked the last drag off his puny little roach. "Damn!" he cursed, flicking the charred remnants into the dirty snow beneath his feet. This semester was supposed to have been a twenty-four-hour party. He'd had an awesome interview at Brown in November, and he was pretty sure his application rocked hard enough to get him in. Plus he was no longer hanging out with little Jenny Humphrey, who was very sweet and had a great rack, but who'd taken up a shitload of his free time. For the rest of senior year Nate had been planning to smoke up, kick back, and just stay mellow until graduation, but without his trusty dealer, that plan was basically moot.

Nate sat back on the green wooden bench and gazed up at the sumptuous limestone apartment buildings lining Fifth Avenue. To his right, he could just see the corner of Blair's Seventy-second Street apartment building. Up in the penthouse, Blair's Russian Blue cat, Kitty Minky, was probably lying stretched out on Blair's rose-colored bedspread, eagerly waiting for Blair to come home and scratch him under the chin with her coral-pink nails. Impulsively, Nate pushed the buttons on his phone to speed-dial Blair's cell phone. It rang six times before she finally picked up.

"Hello?" Blair answered in a clipped voice. She was seated in Garren's new East Fifty-seventh Street salon, which was decorated like a Turkish harem's lair. Gauzy pink-and-yellow silk scarves hung from the ceiling, and huge pink-and-yellow-upholstered pillows were tossed at random around the salon for clients to lounge on and sip Turkish coffee while they waited for their appointments. In front of every stylist's station was an enormous gilt-framed mirror. Gianni, Blair's new hairdresser, had just finished combing out her freshly washed and conditioned locks. With her cell phone pressed against her damp ear, Blair stared at her reflection in the mirror. The critical moment was here: Did she dare go short?

"Hey. It's me, Nate," she heard an old familiar voice murmur in her ear.

Blair was too stunned to answer. They hadn't spoken since New Year's Eve, and even then the conversation had ended badly. What was Nate doing calling her *now*?

"Nate?" Blair replied, half-impatiently, half-curiously. "Is this really important, because I can't really talk. It's kind of a *very* bad time."

"Nah, it's not important," Nate responded as he tried to come up with a reasonable explanation for why he'd called her in the first place. "I just thought you'd want to know I've decided to quit. You know—quit smoking weed." He kicked at a clump of frozen dirt. He wasn't even sure if that was true. Was he *really* quitting? For *good*?

Blair gripped the phone in confused silence on the other end. Nate had always been random—especially when he was stoned—but never *this* random. Gianni tapped his tortoise-shell comb against the back of her chair impatiently. "Well, good for you," she responded finally. "Look, I have to go, okay?"

Blair sounded distracted, and Nate wasn't even sure why he'd called her in the first place. "See you," he mumbled, tucking his phone back into his coat pocket.

"Bye." Blair tossed her silvery pink Nokia phone into her red bowling bag and sat up straight in the leather swivel chair. "I'm ready," she told Gianni, trying to sound confident. "Just remember, I want it short but *feminine*."

Amused creases appeared in Gianni's tanned, intentionally stubbly cheeks. He winked a long-lashed, dark brown eye. "Jes lika Katerina Hepburn. Right?"

Uh-oh.

Blair tightened the belt on her beige salon robe and glared at Gianni's overly pomaded black hair in the mirror, praying he wasn't as stupid and incompetent as he sounded. Maybe it was a just a language thing. "No, *not* Katherine Hepburn. *Audrey* Hepburn. You know, like *Breakfast at Tiffany's*? *My Fair Lady*? *Funny Face*?" Blair searched her brain for a more current celebrity reference, someone with a decent short hair-cut. "Or maybe like Selma Blair," she added desperately, even though Selma's haircut was more tomboyish than what she had in mind.

Gianni didn't respond. Instead, he ran his fingers through Blair's damp brown tresses. "Sucha bee-ootiful 'air," he said wistfully as he picked up his scissors and gathered her hair in his fist. Then, without further ado, he lopped the entire ponytail off with one brutal snip.

Blair closed her eyes as the rope of hair fell to the floor. *Please make me look pretty,* she prayed silently, *and sophisticated and poised and elegant.* She opened her eyes and stared in horror at her reflection. Her wet, blunt, ear-length mop was sticking out in all directions.

"Don't worry," Gianni reassured her as he exchanged his big scissors for a small pair of shears. "Now we shape."

Blair took a deep breath, steeling herself. It was too late to back out of it anyway. Most of her hair was on the floor. "Okay," she gasped. Then her cell phone rang again and she lunged at it. "Wait," she told Gianni. "Hello?"

"Yes, is this Blair Waldorf? Harold's daughter?"

Blair studied herself in the mirror. She wasn't exactly sure *who* she was anymore. She looked more like a new inmate getting her preprison crop than the daughter of notorious corporate lawyer Harold Waldorf, who'd divorced Blair's mother two years ago and now lived in a château in France, where he ran a vineyard with his "life partner," who just happened to be a man.

Considering the turbulent state of her present existence, Blair really wouldn't have minded being someone completely different, which was part of the reason she'd decided to submit herself to Gianni in the first place. She'd even settle for Katherine instead of Audrey as long as the look was totally new.

"Yes," Blair answered feebly.

"Good," the guy on the phone replied. His voice was deep and cajoling, making it hard to guess how old he was. Nineteen or thirty-five? "This is Owen Wells. Your father mentored me at the firm when I was first starting out. We're both Yalies, and I understand you're interested in going there yourself."

Interested? Blair wasn't just *interested* in going to Yale—it was her sole purpose in life. Why the hell else would she be taking *five* APs?

"Yes, I am," she squeaked. She glanced up at Gianni, who was mouthing the words to a cheesy Celine Dion song wafting out of the salon's sound system. "I kind of messed up my interview, though."

Actually, she'd kind of told the interviewer her whole life's sob story and then kind of *kissed* him, which was more than kind of a major "whoops."

"Well, that's exactly why I'm calling," Owen Wells replied, his sexy voice resonating like the bass notes of a cello. "Your father's support means a lot to the school, and they want to give you a second chance. I'm volunteering my services as your alumnus interviewer, and the admissions office has already agreed to use my write-up when they review your application, instead of the interview you did back in November."

Blair was dumbstruck. A second chance—it was almost too good to be true. Tired of waiting, Gianni dropped his scissors on the wheeled cart next to Blair's chair, snatched the latest issue of *Vogue* out of Blair's lap, and minced away to complain about her to his colleagues.

"So when are you available?" Owen Wells persisted.

Now, Blair wanted to say. But she couldn't very well ask Owen to sit and watch Gianni cut her hair while he asked her all those boring stereotypical interview questions like, Who are the most influential people in your life?

"Anytime," she chirped. Then she realized she shouldn't sound *too* desperate, not when she was supposed to be a total whiz kid with an insane schedule. "Actually, today is kind of busy for me and tomorrow might be a little crazy, too. Wednesday or Thursday after school would be better."

"I tend to work pretty late, and I've got meetings up the wazoo this week, but how about Thursday night? Around eight-thirty?"

"Fine," Blair responded eagerly. "Do you want me to come to your office?"

Owen paused. Blair could hear his office chair creak and she imagined him surveying his Philippe Starck–designed Tribeca office with its view of New York Harbor, wondering if it was an appropriate place to meet. She imagined him tall and blond, with a tennis tan, like her father. But Owen Wells would be at least ten years younger than her dad, and so much better looking. She wondered if he knew how cool it was that there was a *w* in each of his names. "Why don't we meet at the Compton Hotel? They've got a nice little bar that should be pretty quiet." He laughed. "I can buy you a Coke, although your father tells me you prefer Dom Pérignon."

Blair's face burned. Her stupid-ass father—what else had he said? "Oh, no, Coke is fine," she stammered.

"Good. I'll see you Thursday night. I'll be wearing my Yale tie."

"I'm looking forward to it." Blair tried to maintain a businesslike tone despite her vivid Owen-at-the-office fantasy. "Thank you so much for calling." She clicked off the phone and looked directly into the gilt mirror in front of her. Her blue eyes already seemed larger and more intense now that she had less hair.

If she were really an actress starring in the movie of her

life—which was what she always liked to imagine—*this* would be the turning point: the day she transformed her look and began rehearsing for the biggest role of her career. She glanced at her watch. There was only half an hour left before she was due back at Constance for gym. There was no reason to rush back, though, especially not when Bendel's was only three blocks away and a new dress for meeting Owen Wells on Thursday night was calling her name. It was absolutely worth getting in trouble for cutting gym if her new haircut and new dress were going to help get her into Yale.

Gianni was drinking coffee and flirting with the shampoo boys. Blair shot him a menacing look, daring him to fuck up her hair.

"Whenever you're ready, miss," he called over in a bored tone, as if he couldn't have cared less if he cut her hair or not.

Blair took a deep breath. She was erasing the past—her failed relationship with Nate, her mother's revolting new husband and embarrassing pregnancy, her botched Yale interview—and recreating herself in a new image. Yale was giving her a second chance, and from now on she would be the master of her own destiny, writing, directing, and starring in the movie that was her life. She could already see the headline in the Styles section of the *New York Times*, featuring her haircut. *Ahead of the* Times: *Gorgeous Brunette Goes Short for Yale Debut!*

Her face broke into the winning smile she was already practicing for her interview with Owen Wells on Thursday night. "I'm ready."

sex poems are full of lies

"So . . . ," Vanessa said, bouncing her knee against Dan's thigh as they lay naked on their backs, contemplating his cracked bedroom ceiling in a postcoital daze. "What did you think?"

Vanessa had already tried sex a couple of times before with her ex-boyfriend Clark, an older bartender she'd gotten together with briefly in the fall, when Dan (along with the rest of the predictable male population) had been too busy mooning over Serena van der Woodsen to notice that Vanessa had fallen in love with him. Even if Vanessa had just done it for the first time, she would have been matter-of-fact about it, because that was the way she was about everything. Dan, on the other hand, wasn't matter-of-fact about anything, and *he* was the one who'd just been deflowered. She couldn't wait to hear his reaction.

"It was . . ." Dan stared unblinkingly up at the gray, turned-off lightbulb dangling from the center of the ceiling, feeling immobilized and overstimulated at the same time. Their hips were touching under the thin, burgundy-colored sheet, and it felt like an electric current was running between them, pinging out of Dan's toes, his knees, his belly button, his elbows, and the ends of his hair.

"Indescribable," he finally answered, because there really were no words to describe how it had felt. Writing a poem about sex would be impossible, unless he resorted to boring, clichéd metaphors like exploding fireworks or musical crescendos. Even those were totally inaccurate. They gave no sense of the actual *feeling*, or how sex was this whole discovery process during which everything commonplace became absolutely amazing. For instance, Vanessa's left arm: it wasn't a particularly spectacular arm—fleshy and pale, covered in brownish fuzz, and sprinkled with moles. While they'd been having sex it had no longer been the same old arm he'd known and loved since he and Vanessa had accidentally gotten locked out of a party in tenth grade—it had been an exquisite, precious thing that he couldn't stop kissing; something new and exciting and delicious. Oh, *God*. See? Everything he could think of to describe what sex was like sounded like a lame ad for a new cereal or something. Even the word *sex* was wrong, and *making love* sounded like a bad soap opera.

Electric would have been a good word to describe what sex was like, but then again, it had too many negative connotations, like the electric chair or an electric cattle fence. *Teeming* was another good word, but what did it mean exactly? And *quivering* sounded too dainty and puny, like a scared little mouse. If he were ever going to write a poem about sex, he wanted to provoke thoughts of sexy, muscular beasts like lions and stags, not mice.

"Earth to Dan?" Vanessa reached over and flicked her finger against his earlobe.

"Pinnacle," Dan muttered senselessly. "Epiphany."

Vanessa ducked under the sheet and blew a giant raspberry on Dan's pale, hollow stomach. "Hello? Are you in shock or something?"

Dan grinned and scooted her up his chest so he could kiss her Cheshire cat mouth and dimpled chin. "Let's do it again."

Whoo!

Vanessa giggled and rubbed her nose against his unruly brown eyebrows. "So I guess you enjoyed it, huh?"

Dan kissed her right eye and then her left. "Mmm," he sighed, his whole body humming with pleasure and desire. "I love you."

Vanessa collapsed on his chest and squeezed her eyes shut. She wasn't a very girly girl, but no girl can help but melt the first time she hears a boy say those three words.

"I love you, too," she whispered back.

Dan felt like his whole body was smiling. Who'd known this mundane Monday in February would wind up so damned . . . *great*?

So much for flowery descriptions and poetic turns of phrase.

All of a sudden his cell phone sounded its startling, vibrating ring from where it sat on the bedside table, only inches away. Dan was pretty sure it was only his little sister, Jenny, calling to complain about school again. He turned his head to read the number on the little screen. PRIVATE, the message flashed, which only happened when Vanessa called him from home.

"It's your sister." Dan propped himself up on one elbow as he reached for his phone. "Maybe she's calling to tell you to get your own damn cell phone, *finally*," he joked. "Should I answer it?"

Vanessa rolled her eyes. She and her twenty-two-year-old bass-guitar-playing sister, Ruby, shared an apartment in the Williamsburg section of Brooklyn. Ruby had made three New Year's resolutions: to do yoga every day, to drink green tea instead of coffee, and to be more nurturing toward Vanessa, since their own parents were too busy being art-hippie freaks up in Vermont to nurture her themselves. Vanessa was pretty sure Ruby was only calling to ask when she'd be home so Ruby could have the meatloaf and mashed potatoes all done when she got there, but it was so unlike Ruby to call Dan's phone right in the middle of the school day that she couldn't resist answering.

She took the ringing phone from Dan and clicked it open. "Yeah? How did you know where to find me?"

"Well, good afternoon to you, darling sister o' mine," Ruby chirped cheerfully. "Remember? I stuck your schedule up on the refrigerator so I'd know exactly where you are and what you're thinking about at all times, like the new and improved version of Big Brothers Big Sisters. Anyway, I just wanted you to know that the mail came and there was a suspicious-looking envelope from NYU addressed to you. I couldn't help but open it. And guess what? *You got in!*"

"No fucking way!" Vanessa's body was already shot through with adrenaline from saying, "I love you," and now *this*. Not to be cheesy, but talk about orgasmic!

She'd never been sure of her chances of getting in early, and just to show the NYU admissions office her artistic range and to prove how serious she was about being a film major, she'd sent them the New York film essay that she'd shot over Christmas break. Once she'd sent it in, she'd worried they'd think she was trying too hard. But now her worries were over. They liked her! They wanted her! Vanessa could finally shake the bitchy, shallow shackles of Constance Billard for good and focus on her craft at a place for serious artists like herself.

Dan was gazing up at her from the bed. His sweet brown eyes seemed to be shining a little less ecstatically than they had been before.

"I'm so proud of you, sweetie," Ruby crooned in her most motherly voice. "Will you be home for dinner? I've been reading Eastern European cookbooks. I'm thinking of making pierogi."

"Sure," Vanessa answered quietly, suddenly concerned about Dan. He hadn't applied anywhere early, so it would be a couple months before he found out where he was going next year. Dan was so sensitive. This was just the sort of thing that could throw him into an insecurity-induced depression, the kind where he locked himself in his room and wrote poems about dying in a car accident or something. "Thanks for letting me know," she told Ruby quickly. "I'll see you later, okay?"

Dan was still staring up at her expectantly as she clicked off the phone and dropped it on the bed. "You got into NYU," he said, trying but failing to hide the note of accusation in his voice. Oh, how skinny and stupid and inadequate he was! Not that he wasn't happy for her, but Vanessa was already into college, and he was just this scrawny guy who liked to write poems and who might never get into college at all. "Wow," he added hoarsely. "That's great."

Vanessa flopped back on the bed and pulled the sheet up around them. The room felt colder now that the sweat of passion had cooled on their bodies. "It's really no big deal," she argued, trying to play down the excitement she'd exuded when she'd heard the news. "You're the one with a poem about to come out in *The New Yorker*."

Over Christmas break, Vanessa had submitted Dan's poem "Sluts" to *The New Yorker* without his knowing, and it had been accepted for publication in the Valentine's Day double issue, which would be out later that week. "I guess," Dan agreed, shrugging his shoulders dubiously. "But I still don't know anything . . . I mean, about my *future*."

Vanessa encircled Dan's waist with her arms and pressed her cheek into his pale, ribby chest. She still couldn't believe she was going to NYU in the fall. It was a sure thing, her destiny. Still trembling with excitement, she tried to focus on consoling Dan. "How many other seventeen-year-old kids have you heard of with poems published in *The New Yorker*? It's amazing," she murmured gently. "And as soon as the admissions officers at the colleges you applied to find out about it, you're going to get in everywhere you applied, and maybe even places you didn't."

"Maybe," Dan responded hollowly. It was easy for Vanessa to sound so confident. She was already *in*.

Vanessa propped herself up on one elbow. There was one sure way of making Dan feel better, at least for a little while. "Remember what we were doing right before Ruby called?" she purred like a mischievous black kitty cat.

Dan frowned up at her. One black eyebrow was cocked at a sultry angle and her pale nostrils were flared. He hadn't thought he'd be up to it anymore, but his body surprised him. He pulled Vanessa down on top of him and kissed her hard. If anything could make a boy feel more like a lion than a mouse, it was a little purring.

Me-ow.

hey people!

Senior slump

I've heard the expression "senior slump" many times, but I never knew what it meant exactly. Now it's crystal clear. Senior slump is when you blow off your afternoon classes and go back to your friend's apartment to order veggie lo mein, drink chardonnay, and smoke cigarettes. It's when you wind up in bed with a boy at three o'clock in the afternoon. It's when you skip third-period calculus to stock up on clingy silk jersey wrap dresses at Diane von Furstenberg's private sale. It's when you accidentally sleep till ten on a Thursday. *Oops.* Last term we were such goody-goodies, teachers' pets. This term we're badasses. We're also feeling our wild oats. I'm pretty sure half the girls in my P.E. class were off kissing boys on the steps of the Metropolitan Museum of Art instead of doing chin-ups on the monkey bars in the gym. Keep it up girls— hooking up is *much* better exercise!

Sightings

J and a tall, freckled girl with an unfortunate haircut giggling during a dance class at Constance Billard. Guess **J** has a new friend. **N** and his buddies ordering chai at **Starbucks**, in the hopes that it might be laced with something mood-altering. **V** at the NYU store buying an NYU mug, an NYU sweatshirt, *and* an NYU baseball cap. And she claims not to be a sucker for that sort of thing. **D** combing his local newsstand for an advance issue of *The New Yorker*. **S** and **A** enjoying a little PDA as usual. She's never had a boyfriend for more than five minutes, so we'll see how long this lasts. . . .

Okay, I admit it. I'm cutting class as we speak. Promise you won't tell!

You know you love me.

gossip girl

s is in love

Standing in a drift of old snow outside the Constance Billard School for Girls on East Ninety-third Street, Aaron Rose waited for Serena to come hurtling through the towering royal blue school doors and into his arms. Mookie, his brown-and-white boxer, sat panting beside him on the sidewalk wearing the red-and-black plaid doggie jacket Serena had bought him yesterday at Burberry. In Aaron's hands were two steaming cups from Starbucks. Ever since they'd gotten together at Serena's wild New Year's Eve party six weeks ago, this had become their little ritual. Aaron would meet Serena after school and they'd amble down Fifth Avenue arm in arm, drinking soy lattes and stopping now and then to kiss. New Year's Eve had been a total fuck-it-we're-both-in-the-mood-so-why-not-hook-up? spontaneous sort of thing, but over the past month they'd spent every out-of-school moment together, and they were now known as the best-looking and most adorable couple—well, threesome, if you included Mookie—on the Upper East Side.

Suddenly a ray of bright winter sun flashed on Serena's cool blond head as she pushed open the school doors, skipped down the stairs in her Stephane Kelian brown suede boots and navy blue Les Best pea coat, and stepped out onto the snowy sidewalk. Her whole face glowed with angelic excitement when she caught sight of Aaron and Mookie.

"Hi, pup!" she squealed as Mookie wriggled up to her and nuzzled her cashmere-gloved hands. She squatted down and let the dog lick her face as she stroked his head. "You look *so* handsome today."

Aaron watched them with a lazy sense of pride. *Yep, that's my girlfriend. Yep, isn't she gorgeous?*

Serena stood up and threw her arms around his neck. The air around them filled with the heady, sandalwood-and-patchouli based scent of the custom-blended essential oil mixture she always wore. "You know what I've been thinking about all day?" she gushed, planting a kiss on Aaron's thin, dark red lips with her full, peach-glossed ones.

Aaron splayed his feet to keep from stumbling backward and spilling the lattes. *"Me?"* he guessed. Serena was the type of girl who gave herself *entirely* to whatever she was into at the moment, and for the time being she just happened to be into Aaron. It had kind of gone to his head.

She closed her eyes and they kissed again, deeply this time. Behind them, girls in neat wool coats and tall leather boots spilled out of the school doors, shouting giddily. A few of them huddled together to watch in awe as Serena and Aaron continued to kiss.

"Oh my God," whispered one eighth grader, swooning in the presence of such coolness. "Do you see what I see?"

Mookie pawed at the snow and whined impatiently. Serena rubbed her cheek against the scratchy alpaca wool of the gray-and-purple sherpa hat she'd bought for Aaron last weekend at Kirna Zabete in Soho. She loved the way his cute dark brown dreadlocks poked out from beneath the earflaps.

Everything about Aaron was so adorable, she just wanted to eat him up with a spoon!

"*Of course* I was thinking about you," she said, taking her latte. She cracked open the lid and blew on the sweet, steaming liquid. "I was thinking we should get tattoos." She paused, waiting for Aaron to respond, but his soft brown eyes looked puzzled, so she went on. "You know, like of our names. To show our commitment to each other." She took a sip of her coffee and licked her lovely, luscious lips. "I've always wanted a tattoo that only I knew about. You know, somewhere *private*."

Aaron smiled hesitantly. He liked Serena a lot. She was intoxicatingly beautiful, a total sweetheart, and completely undemanding. She was above and beyond any girl he'd ever met. But he wasn't sure he wanted to tattoo her name all over his body. In fact, he'd always thought tattoos were kind of violent, like brands on cattle, and as a vegan and a Rastafarian, he was morally opposed to any type of violence.

"Tattoos are against my religion," he stated, but when he saw Serena's gorgeous face crumple in dismay he took her hand and added quickly, "But I'll think about it, okay?"

Serena wasn't one to hold grudges, certainly not against the cutest boy in the universe. Already over it, she tugged on his hand and they started walking toward Fifth Avenue. The sky was a sullen gray, and a chilly wind bit at their faces. In an hour it would be dark.

"So what should we do?" she asked. "I was thinking it might be kind of crazy to go up to the top of the Empire State Building. I've lived here my whole life and I've never even been up there. And it's *so cold*. I bet no one even thinks of going up there at this time of year. It'll be totally empty and romantic, like in a old movie or something."

Aaron laughed. "You've been hanging out with Blair too

much." His stepsister always turned everything into a romantic black-and-white movie from the fifties, trying to make her life even more glamorous than it already was. As they turned down Fifth, Mookie scampered ahead of them, tugging on the leash looped loosely around Aaron's wrist. "Hey, chill out, Mook."

Serena tucked her free hand into Aaron's black North Face parka pocket. "Blair was acting really weird during peer group, that new thing we're doing with the freshmen at lunchtime. After that she just disappeared. She didn't even show up for gym."

Aaron shrugged and sipped his drink. "Maybe she had cramps or something."

Serena shook her pretty head. "I'm worried she's a little jealous. You know, of *us*."

Aaron didn't say anything. Over Christmas he'd developed a huge crush on Blair, even though she was his stepsister. Being with Serena had made him forget all about it, but it was still odd to think that Blair might actually jealous of *them*, when he'd been pining over *her* all those weeks.

"So, are we going to the Empire State Building?" Serena asked, stopping at the next corner and turning to peer back up Fifth Avenue. A fleet of buses roared by. "If we are, we should grab a cab."

Aaron looked at his watch. It was ten after four. "I was kind of thinking I'd like to stop by my house to check the mail." He grinned bashfully, embarrassed by how nerdy he sounded. "Early acceptance letters were mailed this week."

Serena's long-lashed dark blue eyes opened wide. "Why didn't you say so?" She tossed her paper cup in a nearby trash can and took off at a run. "Come on, Mook!" she shouted as the boxer bounded happily after her. "Let's go home and see if your smarty-pants daddy got into Harvard!"

b does j a little favor

Jenny had always been shy and had trouble making friends, but she had managed to make one in peer group that day.

"You know, I never really noticed your, um . . . bra size," Elise murmured shyly as they were packing up their book bags to go home. On either side of them girls slammed their metal locker doors closed and shouted to each other as they ran downstairs and out the school doors.

"Yeah, right," Jenny responded sarcastically, trying to wedge her geometry notebook into her red-and-black-striped Le Sportsac bag in between her French textbook and *Anna Karenina*.

Elise giggled as she wound a fuzzy pink scarf around her neck and buttoned the black velvet buttons on her nerdy tweed coat. She definitely looked like her mother still dressed her in the mornings. "Okay, I noticed. But I never thought it bothered you."

Jenny tucked her curly dark brown hair behind her ears and squinted at Elise. "It *doesn't* bother me."

Elise pulled her fuzzy pink hat down over her blond bob and hitched her backpack up on her shoulder. She was nearly a foot taller than Jenny. "Um, are you busy now? Do you want to, like, do something?"

"Like what?" Jenny zipped up her puffy black parka. Now that she no longer hung out with Nate or her older brother, Dan, she really needed some new friends, and it might be kind of nice to hang out with a girl for once, even though Elise seemed kind of prissy and immature.

"I don't know. Like go buy some new makeup at Bendel's or something?" Elise suggested.

Jenny cocked her head, pleasantly surprised. For a minute there she'd thought Elise was going to suggest buying an ice cream cone or visiting the zoo. "I'd love to," she agreed, slamming her locker door closed and starting to walk toward the stairs. "Come on."

Blair couldn't believe how a simple haircut could change everything so drastically. She'd already tried on every flirty empire-waisted top and A-line skirt Bendel's had in stock—exactly the same types of pieces she'd always worn and looked good in, but now they were all wrong. Her new crop was preppy and sophisticated and gamine. It was going to require a whole new wardrobe.

"From now on I'll wear only solid colors," Blair whispered as she buttoned up her uniform and hung the last unwanted dress on its hanger. "And everything must have a collar." She pulled open the red velvet curtain and dumped six wildly printed Diane von Furstenberg tops into the sales clerk's arms. "I changed my mind. I'm looking for simple suits in navy blue and black. And plain white shirts with collars." She wanted to look sexy in a chic Parisian-woman-wearing-a-simple-black-dress-while-riding-a-bicycle-and-carrying-a-baguette-under-her-arm sort of way. Nate had always had a thing about French girls. He would go out of his way to walk by L'École Française just to gape at the girls in their short gray skirts, high heels, and tight black V-neck sweaters. Those tramps.

Soon Blair had found the first item in her new wardrobe and the perfect thing to wear for her interview Thursday night: a navy blue knit shirtdress by Les Best with a beaded belt and a cute little white lace collar at the neck. It was prim yet intriguing—just what Blair was looking for. She paid for the dress and then headed downstairs to cosmetics to outfit herself with navy blue mascara and a subtle shade of lip gloss that wasn't as girly or come-hither as her usual shade of light pink or dark red.

"Look who's here," Jenny whispered to Elise in front of the Stila counter. "Hi, Blair."

"Great haircut!" added Elise perkily.

Blair turned around to find two of the freshmen from her peer group: she-really-*should*-have-a-breast-reduction Ginny, and in-desperate-need-of-a-makeover Eliza, or whatever their names were, staring at her admiringly. She was horrified to see that they were trying on some of the same eye shadows and lip glosses that she wore all the time. Couldn't they just stick with Maybelline from Rite Aid or something?

Elise frowned down at the vial of glittery black eye dust in her hand. "Is this stuff any good?"

Yes, it's good. But you're really not ready for it yet.

Blair couldn't help but give them a little big-sisterly advice. She slung her brown-and-white-striped Bendel's shopping bag over her wrist and got to work. "With your coloring, I'd go for something lighter." She reached for a sample tube of pale silvery green gel shadow. "This would really bring out the aqua tones in your eyes," she instructed, marveling at how *nice* she sounded.

Elise took the tube and dabbed a little on her eyelids. It

was barely visible, but it caught the light and miraculously made her small, close-together blue eyes look brighter and prettier. "Wow," she trilled, mesmerized.

Jenny reached for the tube. "Can I try?"

Blair snatched it away. "Absolutely not. You need something in beige or peach." Blair couldn't believe herself. The weird thing was, she was enjoying it. "Here." She handed Jenny a fat, rust-colored eye pencil. "It goes on softer than it looks."

Jenny drew a careful line along the edge of one eyelid and blinked at the result. She looked instantly older, and the color gave her big brown eyes a nice amber glow. She leaned forward to do the left one but something in the mirror's reflection caught her eye.

Or some*one*, to be precise.

The store was bustling with shoppers stocking up on winter sale items, but Bendel's only caters to women, so all of the shoppers were female. All but one.

He looked about sixteen, tall and thin, with shaggy blond hair and wearing a chocolate brown corduroy jacket and jeans that hung loose from his gaunt body. Sort of like the guy in the Calvin Klein Eternity for Men ad, except less hunky.

"Wow," Jenny said softly.

"Isn't it great?" Blair chimed in. "Smudge it in a little with your finger. You should use brown mascara, too. It will make your eyes look even bigger."

"No, I mean wow, look at *him*," Jenny clarified. "Behind me."

Blair glanced over her shoulder to see a geeky, too-young-for-her blond boy perusing the Bendel's signature cosmetics bags. She turned back to Jenny. "What? You think he's cute?"

Elise giggled. "He's kind of goofy looking."

Blair's little Help the Hopeless campaign was starting to wear thin. "If he's shopping in Bendel's, he's probably gay. Why don't you just go up and talk to him if you think he's so cute?"

Jenny was mortified. Just go up and start talking to him like some sort of desperate, stalking freak? *No way.*

"Come on," Elise prodded. "You know you want to."

Jenny could barely breathe. Every time she thought she was getting more confident, something like this happened to prove that she was just as insecure as ever. "Maybe we should just leave," she muttered nervously, as if Blair and Elise were about to rope her into participating in some shady drug deal. She picked her book bag up from off the floor. "Thanks for your help," she told Blair quickly. Then she grabbed Elise's hand and dragged her out of the store, keeping her eyes straight ahead as she passed the blond boy.

Pathetic. Blair sighed as she watched them go. But she'd been in such a good mood ever since Owen Wells' call, it wouldn't kill her to give Jenny a little more help when she so obviously needed it. She pulled the receipt for her dress out of her shopping bag and, using the rust-colored eye pencil, drew a big heart on the back of it and wrote Jenny's Constance Billard e-mail address inside it. Everyone's school e-mail addresses were the same, just the first initial and the last name, so it wasn't hard to figure out. Then she crumpled the receipt into a tight little ball and walked past the skinny blond boy, tossing the balled-up receipt hard at his back and spinning through the revolving doors before he had a chance to see who she was.

Blair Waldorf making an effort to do something nice for someone else? Talk about a makeover! This was more than just a Jiffy Lube change of hairstyle. Like a true diva, she was going for the entire weekend spa package, including the spiritual overhaul.

as if he didn't have it good enough already

Just as Aaron had suspected, there was a cream-colored envelope from Harvard waiting for him beside the Spode china milk jug of white roses on the side table in the foyer of his father and stepmother's East Seventy-second Street penthouse apartment. Aaron let an extremely thirsty Mookie tear down the hall to the kitchen with his leash still on and picked up the letter with rigid fingers. Serena was waiting expectantly behind him, but he would really rather have opened it alone. *What if he didn't get in?*

Serena slipped out of her coat and tossed it on the blue toile–upholstered chair in the corner. "I'll still love you no matter what," she said breathlessly.

Aaron stared down at the envelope, annoyed at himself for feeling so tense. He was usually pretty mellow about this kind of thing. "Fuck it," he declared under his breath and tore open the sealed envelope. He unfolded the neatly creased cream-colored piece of paper and read the short paragraph typed on it, twice. Then he looked up at Serena. "Uh-oh."

Her face fell. What a horrible thing for her sweet love to go through! "Oh, poor baby. I'm so sorry."

Aaron handed her the letter and she glanced at it reluctantly.

Dear Mr. Rose, We have reviewed your application and we are very pleased to inform you of your acceptance to Harvard University's class of— Serena's blue eyes were suddenly enormous. "You got in! Oh baby, you got in!"

Behind them, Myrtle, the cook, walked briskly down the hall with a drooling, panting Mookie trailing after her. Her light yellow maid's uniform was spattered with something orangey-red and she looked pissed.

"Myrtle, Aaron got into *Harvard*," Serena announced proudly. She put her arms around her boyfriend and gave him a squeeze. "Isn't that amazing?"

Myrtle was unimpressed. She thrust Mookie's leash at Aaron, her fleshy wrists jangling with gold bracelets and her work-weary hands smelling of onions. "Better take that dog with you where you're going," she chided before stomping back to the kitchen in her new white Nike tennis shoes.

Serena and Aaron grinned mischievously at each other. "I think this calls for a little celebration, don't you?" Aaron asked, his relief mutating instantaneously into cockiness.

Serena tweaked his adorable freckled nose with a slender forefinger. "I know where they keep the champagne."

Blair rode the elevator up to her family's penthouse overlooking Central Park at Seventy-second Street. When the elevator doors rolled open she instantly recognized Serena's new navy blue cashmere pea coat flung carelessly on top of the toile Louis XVI chaise in the foyer. It was still hard to get used to the idea of Serena hanging out at her house when she wasn't even home.

"Blair?" Serena's voice echoed out of the former guest room, which now belonged to Aaron. "Get in here. Where have you been?"

"Hold on," Blair called. She pulled off her light blue duffle coat and hung it up in the coat closet. She didn't really feel like explaining her drastic new look to Serena and Aaron while they were sitting around in their underwear or something equally nauseating, but she didn't see how she could get out of it. If she ignored them, they'd soon be banging her door down, bouncing up and down on her bed, and demanding her attention like immature imbeciles.

The smell of herbal cigarette smoke wafted out into the hall. "Hey," she called, standing outside the half-opened door.

"Come on in," Aaron slurred. After two glasses of Dom Pérignon he was already tipsy. "We're having a party."

Blair pushed open the door. The room had been redecorated for Aaron in shades of aubergine and cerulean, with funky fifties gray metal shutters in the windows instead of curtains and giant vinyl beanbag chairs on the floor to lounge around on. The woven organic hemp mat covering the hardwood floor was littered with CD cases, computer games, DVDs, music magazines, and library books about Jamaican Rasta culture and the evils of the meat industry. Serena and Aaron were sitting on the disheveled Edwardian four-poster bed, drinking champagne out of her mother's best crystal flutes, *in their underwear*, just as Blair had predicted. Actually, Serena was wearing one of Aaron's oversized hunter green BRONXDALE ATHLETIC T-shirts, with her white satin La Perla panties peeking out from underneath it.

Well, at least it was *nice* underwear.

Blair was about to ask what the big occasion was when Serena blurted out, "Aaron got in! He got into Harvard!"

Blair stared at them, bile rising in her throat. It was hard enough to look at Serena's gorgeous abundance of long, pale blond hair now that her own hair was sitting in a trash can back on Fifty-seventh Street, but the smug smile on Aaron's annoying dreadlocked face was enough to make her want to projectile vomit all over his stupid cruelty-free rug.

"Pull up a beanbag," Aaron offered. He pointed to the Harvard mug sitting on his desk. "That mug's pretty clean if you want some champagne."

Serena waved a sheet of cream-colored paper in the air. "Listen to this. 'Dear Mr. Rose,'" she read aloud. "'We have reviewed your application and we are very pleased to inform you of your acceptance to Harvard University's class of—'"

Blair had gone to the hair salon without eating any lunch, and this little we-love-Aaron worshipfest was making her dizzy with disgust. *She* was the one who should have been opening *her* early acceptance letter, but after her botched interview Constance Billard's college advisor had told her it was best not to apply early. Getting into Yale had been Blair's sole mission in life—well, besides marrying Nate Archibald and living happily every after in the ivy-covered brick town house just off Fifth that she already had picked out—but now she'd have to wait until April along with all the rest of the morons in her class to find out if she'd even gotten in. It was completely unfair.

"Sorry, Blair." Aaron sipped his champagne. He'd always been supersensitive about ruffling Blair's feathers, but he was feeling too good about himself right now to bother. "I'm not going to apologize for getting in. I deserve this."

As if the enormous new science wing his father's development company built on campus last year had absolutely nothing to do with it.

"Fuck you," Blair replied. "In case you forgot, I would be hearing from Yale right now if you hadn't kept me up drinking shit beer and eating crappy junk food in that gross motel room the night before my interview."

Aaron rolled his eyes. "I never told you to kiss your interviewer."

Serena let out a little snort and Blair glared at her.

"Sorry," Serena apologized quickly. "Come on, Blair," she coaxed. "You're, like, the best student in our class. You're totally getting in. You just have to wait until April to find out."

Blair kept on glaring at her. She didn't want to wait until April. She wanted to know *now*.

Aaron lit another herbal cigarette and tilted his chin toward the ceiling to blow a few smoke rings. Already there seemed to be a sort of lazy, superior air about him, as if he knew he could just drink champagne all day for the rest of second semester and still go to Harvard. The fucker.

"Hey," he yawned. "I have to head up to Scarsdale to practice with my band, but let's go out later to celebrate."

Serena stood up on the bed and did a few jumping jacks, as if she really needed the exercise. "Definitely."

Blair watched Serena's gorgeous hair fly up into the air above her head and then cascade prettily down onto her shoulders as Aaron blew more smoke rings. All of a sudden, Blair couldn't stand to be in the same room with them. "I have homework to do," she huffed, reaching up to feel her new hairdo as she turned to leave.

"Oh my God!" Serena cried, vaulting off of Aaron's bed. "Wait, Blair—your *hair*!"

Nice of her to finally notice.

Blair stopped in the doorway and put a hand to where her dark hair fell in a clean line at the nape of her neck. "I like it," she declared defensively.

Serena walked around her like she was one of those Greek marble statues on the main floor of the Met. "Oh my God!" she repeated and reached out to tuck a flyaway hair behind

Blair's ear. "I *love* it!" she exclaimed, a little too enthusiastically.

Blair wrinkled her pert nose suspiciously. Did Serena really love it, or was she just being fake? It was always so hard to tell.

"You look exactly like Audrey Hepburn," Aaron remarked from the bed.

Blair knew he was only saying what she wanted to hear to make up for being such a smug asshole about getting into Harvard. She thought about mentioning her Yale alum interview with Owen Wells on Thursday night but decided to keep the interview to herself. "Excuse me," she told them coldly. "I have stuff to do."

Serena watched Blair leave and then climbed back onto the bed beside Aaron. She picked up the letter from Harvard and folded it up, carefully tucking it inside the envelope again. "I'm so proud of you," she murmured, falling into Aaron's arms and kissing him.

Eventually Aaron pulled away, but Serena kept her eyes closed, licking the sweet herbal aftertaste of his kiss from her lips. "I love you," she heard herself say. The words seemed to have just fallen out of her mouth. She opened her eyes dreamily.

Aaron had never told a girl he loved her, and he hadn't planned to say it to Serena, at least not right away. But it had already been an amazing day, and she was so completely gorgeous with her cheeks all flushed and her perfect mouth all red from kissing. Why not? It was like the end of one of his secret cheesy rock-star fantasies, where he and some incredibly hot girl roared off into the sunset together on a kick-ass Harley.

"I love you, too," he said back, and kissed her again.

gossipgirl.net

topics ◄ *previous*   *next* ►   *post a question*   *reply*

hey people!

Aren't we special?

So the rumor floating around about the Ivies not accepting anyone early this year turned out to be totally false. Hooray—some of us got in! I know we're feeling pretty special, but if we start partying like it's 2099, drinking champagne before homeroom and cutting half our classes, we're going to wind up with only each other to party with, because all our other friends are going to hate our guts. Try to keep it to yourselves if you can, at least until April when the rest of the class finds out where they're going. It's for your own good, I promise.

The *L* word

With Valentine's Day less than a week away, love is in the air *everywhere*. It's on the tips of our tongues. It's what we're thinking about before we fall asleep. We catch ourselves and our neighbors doodling corny hearts in math class. But just because the world has turned into one gigantic Be Mine candy heart doesn't mean we have to go around making promises we can't keep. Using the *L* word in intimate settings can be dangerous. I prefer to use it more generally, as in, *I love you all*. And I mean that, I really do!

Sightings

N skulking down **Madison Avenue** with his hands in his coat pockets, looking uncharacteristically tense and preoccupied. **V** and **D** kissing in **Shakespeare Books**, near **NYU**—*aw, how* cute. **B** at **Sigerson Morrison** in **NoHo,** trying on pair of shoes in the store. **S** in **Fetch** on

Bleecker Street, buying another irresistible doggie outfit for her favorite pooch. **J** and her new friend, **E**, giggling in the feminine-hygiene aisle at Duane Reade. Ah, youth. And **A**, stocking up on used reggae records at a tiny unnamed shop on East Third Street. He's got to have something to listen to while he blows off the rest of second semester.

Your e-mail

Dear GG,
I heard that dealer who used to work in the pizza place got busted by the NYPD and now he's doing time as a narc in the park, busting all his old customers.
—Dawg

Dear Dawg,
That sounds like a bad TNT movie. I just hope none of our friends end up starring in it.
—GG

Dear GossipG,
I totally forgot to tell you before, but I saw that little freshman with the giant boobs in the waiting room of my cosmetic surgeon. She was looking at a book called *Celebrity Breasts*. I'm serious. Like, totally choosing which ones she was going to get.
—tattletail

Dear tattle,
That's all very interesting, but pray tail—I mean tell—why were *you* there?
—GG

As if you weren't already excited enough . . .

Now that the early admissions thing is over, we can focus on something truly important: Fashion Week. It starts this Friday, and all my favorite people will be there, including me. See you in the front row!

You know you love me.

gossip girl

scrawny westside poet has first taste of fame

On his way to Riverside Prep Tuesday morning, Dan stopped at the newsstand on Seventy-ninth and Broadway to buy the Valentine's Day issue of *The New Yorker* and a large black coffee that tasted like it had been made three years ago—just the way he liked it. The cover of *The New Yorker* was an illustration of Noah's Ark docked at a pier in New York Harbor, with the Statue of Liberty looming in the background. The words *The Love Boat* were painted on the side of the ark, and all of the animals lined up to board were holding hands and kissing and groping each other. It was pretty funny. Dan stood on the corner and lit an unfiltered Camel with trembling fingers as he turned back the cover and searched the table of contents for his poem. There it was under Poems: Daniel Humphrey, page forty-two, "Sluts." He flipped to it, forgetting all about the burning cigarette propped between his lips. Page forty-two happened to be the ninth page of a fourteen-page story by Gabriel Garcia Rhodes called "Amor con los Gatos"—"Love with Cats"—and right there, in the middle of the story, was Dan's poem.

Wipe the sleep from my eyes and pour me another cup.
I see what you've been trying to tell me all along,

Shaving your head and handling me (so delicately)
With satin and lace:
You're a whore.

It was freezing outside, but nervous sweat beaded on Dan's eyelids, and his tongue was as dry as firewood. Dan spat the burning cigarette out onto the sidewalk and closed the magazine, tucking it into his black messenger bag. If he'd turned to the Contributors page, he would have seen the entry: *Daniel Humphrey (Poem, p. 42) is a high-school senior in New York City. This is his first published work.* But Dan couldn't handle looking at the magazine for a moment longer, not when thousands of people were right now browsing through it and stopping to read his brutal, angry poem, which he honestly wasn't sure was any good.

Dan walked down Broadway toward school, his hands shaking crazily. If only he could have pulled off some heist like sabotaging *The New Yorker*'s printing presses so they couldn't print vowels anymore. Then all the Valentine's Day issues would have been recalled from the newsstands late last night.

As if he could ever have pulled *that* off.

"Yo, dude," Dan heard the familiar, conceited voice of his least-favorite Riverside Prep classmate behind him. Dan stopped walking and turned around to see Chuck Bass flipping his signature navy blue monogrammed cashmere scarf over one shoulder and running his manicured fingers through his brown-and-blond highlighted hair. "Nice poem in *The New Yorker*, man." He gave Dan a congratulatory clap on the shoulder, his monogrammed pinky ring glittering in the winter sunlight. "Who knew you were such a stud?"

Was there something distinctly *gay* about Chuck Bass these days? Or perhaps not. Just because he'd gotten blond highlights and was wearing a slim, cream-colored wool coat by Ralph Lauren *and* orange leather Prada sneakers didn't mean he'd given up molesting defenseless, drunken girls at parties. Perhaps he was simply expressing himself.

There's certainly nothing wrong with that.

"Thanks," Dan mumbled as he fiddled with the plastic top on his coffee cup. He wondered if Chuck was planning on walking all the way to school with him so they could discuss his poem. But then Dan's cell phone rang, saving him from having to answer Chuck's inane questions about how many chicks he'd bagged before writing the poem, or whatever Chuck Bass liked to talk about on his way to school in the mornings.

Dan put the phone to his ear and Chuck clapped him on the shoulder again and kept walking.

"Hello?"

"Congratulations, Danielson!" Rufus shouted into the phone. His father never got out of bed before eight o'clock, so this was the first time Dan had spoken to him all morning. "You're the real banana, the genuine article! *The New Yorker*, the goddamned *New Yorker*!"

Dan chuckled, feeling slightly ashamed. Countless notebooks filled with his father's odd, disjointed poems were stashed in a dusty box in the broom closet. Even though he was an editor of lesser-known Beat poets, the truth was, Rufus had never actually been published.

"And you'll never believe—," Rufus continued, but then his voice broke off. Dan heard the toilet flush in the background. Typical. His dad had been talking to him while he was in the can.

Dan gulped his coffee and picked up his pace, crossing Broadway and heading down Seventy-seventh Street. He was going to be late for first-period chemistry if he didn't hurry up. Not that that would be such a bad thing. "Dad? You still there?" he asked.

"Hold on, kid," Rufus replied distractedly. "I got my hands full here."

Dan could picture his dad drying his hands on the frayed red towel hanging on the back of the bathroom door and then pulling his rolled-up copy of *The New Yorker* out from under his hairy arm so he could read Dan's poem again.

"The deans of admissions from Brown and Columbia just called to tell me what a prodigy you are," Rufus explained. It sounded like his mouth was full of something, and Dan could hear water running. Was he brushing his teeth? "They were slobbering all over themselves, the greedy bastards."

"Brown and Columbia? Really?" Dan repeated in disbelief. Ahead of him the sidewalk, shopfronts, and pedestrians suddenly all blurred together into a slow-moving, oceanic mass. "Are you sure it was them? Columbia and Brown?"

"As sure as my piss is still yellow," Rufus answered blithely.

Usually Dan blanched at his father's crudeness, but right now he was too preoccupied with his own success. Maybe being a published poet wouldn't be such a bad thing after all. Ahead of him the black metal doors of Riverside Prep's upper-school entrance loomed before him. "Hey Dad, I have to get to class, but thanks for calling. Thank you for *everything*," he gushed with a rush of affection for his belligerent old dad.

"That's all right, kid. Don't let this go to your head, though," Rufus joked, unable to hide the pride in his gruff voice. "Remember, poets are a humble bunch."

"I'll remember," Dan promised earnestly. "Thanks again, Dad."

He clicked off and pushed open the school doors, waving to Aggie, the ancient front-desk receptionist who wore a different wig every day of the week, as he signed in. His cell phone beeped and he realized he'd missed a call while he'd been talking to his father. Cell phones were forbidden during school hours, but first period had already begun and the halls were empty. Trudging up the concrete stairs on the way to the chemistry lab, he called his voice-mail.

"Daniel Humphrey, this is Rusty Klein from Klein, Lowenstein & Schutt. I read your poem in *The New Yorker* and, assuming you don't have an agent yet, I'm going to represent you. I've got you on the guest list for the Better Than Naked show Friday night. Let's talk then. You may not know it yet, but you're hot shit, Daniel. The public needs a serious young poet to make them feel worthless and superficial. And now that we've got their attention, we'd sure as hell better keep the momentum going. You're the next Keats, and we're going to make you so famous so fast, you'll think you were born that way. Looking forward to it. Ciao!"

Dan wobbled outside the door of the chemistry lab as he listened to Rusty Klein's loud, breathless message for a second time. He'd heard of Rusty Klein. She was the agent who'd negotiated the million-dollar book deal for the Scottish jockey who'd claimed to be Prince Charles' illegitimate son. Dan had read about it in the *New York Post*. He had no idea what the Better Than Naked show was, but it was pretty cool of Rusty to put him on the guest list for it when they'd never even met. He also loved being called the next Keats. Keats was one of his major influences, and if Rusty Klein could recognize *that* after reading only one of his poems, he definitely wanted her to represent him.

Tucking his phone back into his bag, he pulled out his

copy of *The New Yorker* again. This time he turned to the Contributors page, reading his short bio before he turned to his poem on page forty-two. He read the poem from start to finish, no longer ashamed to see his own work in print. Rusty Klein thought he was good—*Rusty Klein*! So maybe it was true. Maybe he *was* good. He looked up and peeked through the little window in the chemistry lab door at the row of boys' heads, all lined up like chess pieces facing the blackboard. School suddenly seemed so trivial. He was on to phenomenally bigger and infinitely better things!

Suddenly the lab door swung open and the bizarrely short Mr. Schindledecker stood gazing up at Dan, wearing an ugly double-breasted suit and pulling on his wiry brown mustache. "Are you planning to join us, Mr. Humphrey, or would you rather stay out here and watch through the window?"

Dan rolled up his copy of *The New Yorker* and tucked it under his arm. "I think I'll join you," he replied, stepping inside the lab and walking calmly to a seat at the back of the room. How strange. Dan never did anything calmly, and he'd barely recognized his voice when he'd spoken just now, for in it was a brazen note of cockiness, as if something new inside of him had blossomed and was ready to be let loose.

It was like that line in the Keats poem, "Why Did I Laugh Tonight?" *Verse, Fame, and Beauty are intense indeed. . . .*

And Dan was definitely feeling it.

the scoop on the stoop

"Let's go outside and smoke cigarettes," Elise whispered in Jenny's ear as they headed down to the cafeteria for recess, Constance Billard's 11 A.M. juice-and-cookies break. Only second-semester seniors were allowed to leave school during recess, so she was very clearly proposing something completely illegal.

Jenny stopped on the stairs. "I didn't know you smoked."

Elise unzipped the small outside pocket of her beige Kenneth Cole backpack and pulled a pack of Marlboro Lights halfway out. "Only every once and a while," she replied, pushing the pack back inside in case a teacher came down the stairs. "Are you coming?"

Jenny hesitated. If the receptionist noticed them leaving, she might yell at them and then call their homeroom teacher or even their parents. "How—?"

"Let's just *go*," Elise urged, tugging on Jenny's hand. She started to run down the stairs, pulling Jenny after her. "Go, go, *go*!"

Jenny held her breath as she followed Elise downstairs and sprinted across the red-carpeted reception hall toward the front doors. Trina, the school receptionist, was barking into her headset and sorting the mail at the same time. She didn't even notice the two freshman girls streak past without stopping to sign out.

Blair sat alone on the East Ninety-fourth Street stoop favored by the Constance Billard senior girls, furiously smoking a Merit Ultra Light and running through the college interview questions she'd been prepared to answer since October. There were only two days left until her interview with Owen Wells, and she absolutely refused to fuck this one up.

Tell me about your interests. What kinds of things are you involved in after school?

I'm president of the French club and the social services board at school. I'm also a peer group leader, counseling freshmen on social issues. I'm nationally ranked in tennis—I play all summer, but only twice a week during the winter. I volunteer in soup kitchens whenever I can. I also chair the organizing committees for about eight charity functions a year. We were going to do a Valentine's Day ball this Sunday to benefit Little Hearts, a charity for children with heart problems, but the ball got canceled because of Fashion Week. We were worried no one would come. I sent a letter to everyone on the guest list and still raised almost $300,000. Fundraising has always been one of my particular strengths, and I definitely plan to volunteer my services at Yale.

Blair could just imagine Owen's eyes widening in impressed surprise. How could Yale *not* accept her? She was first class.

A first-class liar is more like it. The whole soup kitchen thing is completely bogus, and she'd sort of skipped the part about the seven *other* chairpeople who'd helped raise the money for Little Hearts.

"Hey Blair!"

Serena was ambling down the sidewalk toward her, wearing black fishnets with a hole in one knee, her luminous blond hair pulled up in a messy bun. For some girls this would have been a very white-trash moment, but for Serena it was an I-can-get-away-with-this-because-I-look-good-in-anything moment. A cab rushed down the street and the driver whistled out the window and honked as he drove by. Serena was so used to the sound of men whistling and cars honking, she never even bothered to turn around.

She sat down next to Blair and pulled a crumpled turquoise-colored pack of American Spirits out of her pocket. She'd started smoking them when she and Aaron had gotten together, because they were supposed to be all natural and additive-free.

As if there's such a big difference between all-natural carbon monoxide and fake carbon monoxide. Get real.

"I still can't believe how cool you look," Serena breathed, admiring Blair's hairdo as she lit her cigarette. "Who knew you'd look so *hot* with short hair."

Blair touched her head self-consciously. She'd thought she was supposed to be mad at Serena but now she couldn't even remember why. Her haircut *was* hot, if she did say so herself.

Flattery can work wonders.

"So, I've been trying to think of a good present to get for Aaron, you know, to congratulate him on getting into Harvard? Can you think of anything he really wants, or maybe something he needs?"

Now Blair remembered why she was mad at Serena. *Aaron, Aaron, Aaron.* It was boring to the point of utter nausea. "Not really," she yawned in response. "A makeover?"

"Very funny," Serena replied. "Hey, don't we know those girls?"

Across the street, Jenny and Elise were walking in that self-conscious, bumping-into-each-other way fourteen-year-old girls have of approaching people they're embarrassed to talk to.

Eventually the two girls bumbled across the street. "We brought our own cigarettes," Jenny announced as nonchalantly as she could, still a little freaked out that she'd just sneaked out of school.

Elise pulled a pack of Marlboros out of her bag, but before she could offer one to Jenny, Serena tossed over her pack of American Spirits. "Put those away. These are so much better for you."

Elise nodded her head seriously. "Thanks." She pulled two cigarettes out of the pack and stuck them both between her lips. Then she flicked on her mint green Bic lighter, puffing on them simultaneously before handing one to Jenny.

Jenny sucked on it hesitantly. After Nate had broken up with her, she'd tried to take up smoking as part of her new jaded-woman image, but they'd given her such bad sore throats, she'd had to quit after only a few days.

"So, have you checked your e-mail today?" Blair asked her, cocking a freshly plucked eyebrow mysteriously.

Jenny coughed out a lungful of smoke. "My e-mail?"

Blair smirked to herself. Even though that blond boy in Bendel's had been kind of dorky looking, he and Jenny would make a very cute couple. The beanpole and the big-breasted cutie-pie. "Forget it," she replied even more mysteriously. "Just be sure to check it regularly from now on."

Of course now Jenny wanted to sprint back to school to check out her e-mail, but she couldn't just abandon Elise, especially not when two more senior girls were walking toward the stoop to join the smoking party.

"My fucking feet are killing me in these boots. It's like Japanese foot binding." Kati Farkas plopped herself down beside Blair and unzipped her peacock blue Charles Jourdan ankle boots.

"*Stop* whining about those boots," Kati's glued-together-at-the-hip friend Isabel Coates moaned. Isabel leaned against the stoop's metal railing and took a sip from a paper cup full of whipped cream–topped hot chocolate. She was wearing a Kelly green Dolce & Gabbana coat from a weekend sample sale. It was buttonless and tied at the waist with a thick black cord, like a Kelly green monk's robe.

No wonder it never sold out back in October.

"Maybe if you got some Japanese foot binding *done* those boots wouldn't hurt so much," Isabel continued. "Or if you'd let *me* buy them instead of you, since *I'm* the one who saw them first."

"Chinese," Jenny couldn't help but correct. "The Chinese used to bind women's feet."

Kati and Isabel stared at her blankly. "Shouldn't you be in school?" Isabel demanded.

"They're smoking with us," Blair said protectively. It was kind of fun having two little ninth-grade sisters. Not that she ever wanted a *real* little sister or anything.

Kati pretended not to notice that Blair was actually being nice to these two little snot-nosed fourteen-year-olds and threw her arms around Blair's neck instead, kissing her on each Stila-powdered cheek.

Mwah! Mwah!

"I can't believe I haven't said anything, but your hair looks totally *gorg*. I just love, love, *love* it!" she squealed. "You were so brave. I heard you got gum in it. Is that why you decided to go so short?"

"Can I touch it?" asked Isabel. She put down her hot chocolate and reached out to pat the back of Blair's head with a tentative hand. "It feels so weird! Like a boy!"

Blair suddenly wished she'd worn a hat or some sort of turban to school. She dropped her cigarette on the step below her and squashed it with the pointy toe of her boot. "Come on, you guys," she beckoned, rising to her feet and holding out her gloved hands to Jenny and Elise like Mary Poppins collecting the children at the playground. "I'll walk you back to school."

Jenny and Elise tossed their cigarettes into the shrubbery in front of the brownstone next door and stood up, hitching their bags up on their shoulders. Now that they'd tried smoking cigarettes with the seniors on a freezing-cold stoop, they weren't exactly sure what the attraction was.

"Do you think my hair would look good that short?" Elise asked, hurrying to keep up with Blair.

Anything would have been an improvement on the my-first-haircut bob Elise was presently sporting, but Blair didn't have the heart or the energy to tell her. "I'll give you my stylist's number," she offered generously.

As they turned down East Ninety-third Street, Mary, Vicky, and Cassie burst through the doors and waved to them.

"We saw you leave at recess!"

"We came out to get you!"

"We didn't want you to get in trouble!"

Blair put her arms around Jenny and Elise and herded them toward the school doors, wise to the fact that the three girls were just being obnoxiously nosy. "We're fine," she told them coolly. "Shouldn't you be in class?"

Mary, Vicky, and Cassie stared after them in hurt disbelief. They were *so* much cooler than Jenny and Elise. What did they have to do to prove it?

Serena remained on the chilly stoop, not exactly thrilled that she'd been left alone with Kati and Isabel. She examined her split ends, trying to come up with the perfect you-got-into-college! gift for Aaron while Kati and Isabel waited eagerly for the real scoop on Blair's hair.

"Did she have lice or something?"

"I heard she had this manic depressive fit and hacked it off with a nail scissors. She had to go to the salon to fix it."

"I think it looks cool," Serena answered dreamily in reply.

Kati and Isabel glared at her, disappointed. If Serena wasn't going to dish anything out, they'd just have to make something up.

And let's be honest—that sounds like *much* more fun.

Disclaimer: All the real names of places, people, and events have been altered or abbreviated to protect the innocent. Namely, me.

hey people!

The premature male midlife crisis

What's with **C**'s *highlights*? Sure, they sort of match his stretchy pastel shirts and orange Prada sneakers, but since when was he so . . . outré? I also heard he was seen on Monday night dancing at a new red-rope, guest-list-only club in Greenwich Village called **Bubble**, a very boys-only kind of scene, if you know what I mean. Could it be that since he's already hit on every female in the city, he's moved on to the males?

The other boy I'm a little concerned about is **N**, my personal favorite. Yes, he's still as hot as ever, and yes, I would give up my Hermès Birkin bag to be his fairy princess. I just wish he'd stop lurking around upper Fifth Avenue taking surreptitious slurps from that silver flask he keeps in his pocket and looking like a nervous wreck. If he needs a hand to hold, he knows where to find me.

But the greatest transformation of all is in skinny, scruffy **D**. If you haven't seen him since this morning, this is breaking news: he got a haircut! It's definitely the work of the old man barber on Broadway and West Eighty-eighth, but his sweet brown eyes are actually visible now, which is definitely an improvement, and there seems to be some sexy-literary-dude sideburn action happening, too. He's got it going on!

Hanging out with the big girls

It's extremely flattering to be taken under the wing of an older girl and given a glimpse of the we're-so-cool-we-don't-even-have-to-think-about-trying side of life. But don't get carried away, thinking said older girl is going to start asking you out to the movies. She's not. And as soon as she gets too busy with APs and parties and shopping for sandals, or whatever it is older girls do in their spare time, she's going to forget about all those groovy times you had together. She might even forget your name. Of course, I could be totally wrong. Maybe you'll wind up friends for life and sponsor each other at the Connecticut country club you both join when you're married with kids. Or not. Don't say I didn't warn you.

Your e-mail

 Dear GG,
So I may have misread what was going on, but I'm pretty sure I saw A from Bronxdale with this other girl in our class, and he was all, "I'm the man, I'm into Harvard," and she was all, "You're so hot. I want you." Um, doesn't he have a girlfriend?
—S.I.B.

 Dear S.I.B.,
What does S.I.B. stand for, anyway? Seeing is believing? Sad in Biloxi? Small is beautiful? If what you say is true, I'm S.F.A.C.B.—sad for a certain blond.
—GG

 Dear Ggirl,
I heard B got caught doing drugs in school and now she secretly has to do community service. She's going to rehab, too, which is why she cut all her hair off. They make you do that, like, in prison.
—Daisy

 Dear Daisy,
It sounds like a bad made-for-Lifetime special. You don't really believe all that, do you?
—GG

Oops. I'm late for my fake-tan rubdown at Bliss—it's the *only* way to stay smiling till summer!

You know you love me.

gossip girl

n buys a dime bag

On Tuesday after school, Nate wandered into Central Park to check out the dealers in Sheep Meadow. He'd gone a full twenty-four hours without getting high, and instead of feeling healthy and energized, he was bored out of his drug-free mind. His classes at school seemed twice as long, and even Jeremy Scott Tompkinson's lame-ass fart jokes barely made him crack a smile.

The late afternoon sun hung low in the sky, casting an eerie golden glow on the frozen brown grass in the meadow. Two heavyset guys dressed in black sweatshirts with the word *Staff* printed on the back were passing a football back and forth, and a tiny old woman wearing a red Chanel suit and a fox fur stole was walking her freshly groomed bichon frise. As usual, the dealers were all sitting on benches around the perimeter of the meadow, listening to WFAN on their Discmans or reading the *Daily News*. Nate spotted a familiar redheaded guy dressed in a light gray Puma tracksuit with matching gray-and-white Puma sneakers, gray wraparound shades, and a fuzzy black Kangol hat.

"Hey Mitchell!" Nate called delightedly. Damn, it was good to see him. Mitchell raised his hand in greeting as Nate walked over. "I thought you were in Amsterdam, man."

Mitchell shook his head slowly. "Not yet."

"I've been looking for you. I was almost going to buy from one of those other dirtbags. You're carrying, right?" Nate asked.

Mitchell nodded and stood up. They began walking down the pathway together, just two friends taking a stroll in the park. Nate pulled a folded-up hundred-dollar bill from his coat pocket and held it in his fist, ready to slip it into Mitchell's palm as soon as he passed over the goods.

"I got a new shipment in from Peru," Mitchell said, pulling a plastic baggie of pot out of his pocket and handing it discreetly to Nate.

If you happened to be in the park watching them, you might have thought they were just sharing a snack or something. That is, if you were completely naïve.

"Thanks, man." Nate handed over the hundred and tucked the plastic baggie into his coat pocket, breathing out a deep, relieved breath. Too bad he didn't have any rolling papers with him or he would have rolled up a big fatty right then and there. "So," he said, figuring it was only polite to make some casual conversation with Mitchell before taking off. "You still moving to Amsterdam or what?"

Mitchell stopped walking and unzipped his Puma jacket. "Nah. I'm stuck here for a while." He pulled up his gray thermal shirt to reveal his bare, freckled chest. There were wires taped to it.

Nate had seen *Law & Order* enough times to know what those wires meant. The bleak scenery seemed to close in on him, and he stumbled backwards. Had he blacked out or something? Was this all a bad dream?

Mitchell let his shirt drop and zipped his jacket up again. He took a step toward Nate, as if he was worried Nate would try to make a break for it. "Sorry, kid. They got me. I'm working for the man now." He jerked his head at the benches behind them. "Those 'dirtbags' on the bench are all cops, okay, so don't try to run. You and I are going to wait here until I give the sign, and then one of them is going to walk you down to the precinct on Amsterdam. *Amsterdam*—pretty ironic, huh?"

Nate could tell Mitchell was trying to get him to smile so the dealer wouldn't have to feel so bad for busting him. "Okay," Nate said woodenly. How had this happened? He'd never been double-crossed before, and it was a pretty crappy feeling. He dropped the baggie of pot on the ground and kicked it away from him. "*Shit*," he swore under his breath.

Mitchell picked up the baggie and put his hand on Nate's shoulder. He raised his free hand in the air and waved to the cops on the benches. Two guys stood up and hurried over. They didn't even look like cops. One of them was wearing black Club Monaco jeans and the other was wearing a stupid red pom-pom hat. They flashed their badges at Nate.

"We're not going to cuff you," Club Monaco explained. "You're a minor, right?"

Nate nodded sullenly, avoiding the cop's gaze. He didn't turn eighteen until April.

"When we get to the precinct you can call your parents."

I'm sure they'll be thrilled, Nate thought bitterly.

Across the meadow the two guys playing football and the old lady and her fluffy white dog were all huddled together, watching Nate getting busted like it was the first episode of some hot new reality show.

"You'll be out in a couple hours," the red pom-pom cop said, writing something in a notebook. Nate noticed the cop was wearing gold hoop earrings and he realized she was a woman, despite her broad shoulders and thick-fingered hands. "They'll fine you and probably give you mandatory rehab."

Mitchell kept his hand on Nate's shoulder as if to offer moral support. "You're lucky," he added.

Nate kept his head down, hoping no one he knew would see him. He didn't feel very lucky.

introducing the new d

Tuesday afternoon, Vanessa stood outside Riverside Prep, filming the frozen remains of a dead pigeon carcass and thinking about sex while she waited for Dan to appear. Dan had left a message for her at the reception desk at Constance Billard to come and meet him after school. *Urgent. Meet me here at four,* it said. *What a freak,* Vanessa thought lovingly. What could possibly be so urgent? He was probably just having an attack of paranoia because his poem had come out in *The New Yorker* today. Either that or he was feeling extremely stimulated and couldn't *wait* to do it again. Before even taking a shower that morning Vanessa had run downstairs and bought six *New Yorker*s from the newsstand on the corner. That way there would always be a spare copy to wave in Dan's face when he was feeling especially inadequate.

When she really thought about it, *she* was the one who should have been freaking out. The poem was all about a guy feeling insecure around women, particularly his dominating girlfriend. People who knew them were going to think Vanessa was a real ball-breaker. But the last line was so sweet and sexy, she couldn't really complain.

Take care of me. Take me. Take care. Take me.

Reading it made her want to rip off all her clothes and jump him. *Gently*, of course.

Just then Dan burst through the black doors of Riverside Prep practically in midsentence. He waved his rumpled copy of *The New Yorker* at Vanessa and galloped up to her in his worn-out white Pumas and navy blue cords, planting a sloppy, wet kiss on her mouth. "This has been the best day of my life!" he trumpeted. "I love you!"

"You don't have to be romantic to get in my pants again," Vanessa giggled and kissed him again. "I'm always available. And by the way, I love you, too."

"Cool." Dan smiled goofily back at her.

Vanessa couldn't believe this was the same old Dan she'd seen only yesterday. He was still pale, thin, and overcaffeinated, but his brown eyes were shining and there were traces of smiley-face dimples in his usually sallow cheeks. Wait a minute. Since when could she actually see his eyes? "Whoa, you got a haircut," she observed, standing back to check it out.

Dan had asked the barber to cut his hair short with long sideburns, figuring the sideburns would keep him from looking like all the preppy assholes in his class. He swept his hand over his head self-consciously. It felt odd, but somehow cleaner than before, more . . . *homogenous*. And that was exactly what he wanted—to be judged by his work, not his hair.

Whatever you say, Sideburn Man.

Vanessa put her hands on the hips of her black parka coat. Something about Dan's haircut was so deliberate, like he was actually going for a certain artsy, bohemian look instead of just stumbling upon one by mistake. "It's different," she mused, already feeling a little nostalgic for the old scruffy-haired Dan. "I guess I'll get used to it."

Behind them a group of eighth-grade boys spilled out the

school doors singing "Hello Dolly" at the top of their lungs. They'd just been released from music class and were still too young and innocent to realize how gay they sounded.

Hello, Dolly! Well hel-loo, Dolly!
It's so nice to have you back where you belong!

Dan pulled a pack of unfiltered Camels out of his black messenger bag, tipped one out, and stuck it between his lips. His fingers trembled wildly as he lit it. Well, at least *that* hadn't changed. He offered the pack to Vanessa. "Want one?"

Vanessa stared at him and chuckled in disbelief. "Since when do I smoke?"

Dan exhaled into the air above her head and rolled his eyes. "Sorry. I don't know why I just did that." He shoved the pack back into his bag and grabbed Vanessa's frozen fingers. "Come on. Let's walk somewhere. I have something major to tell you."

As they were taking off, Zeke Freedman walked out of school bouncing a neon blue basketball. Zeke was big and lumbering, but he was Riverside Prep's star basketball player. He'd grown out his curly black hair so it hung down to his shoulders, and he was sporting a new slate gray snowboarding jacket. Zeke and Dan had been best friends since second grade, but they hadn't really hung out in the last few months because Dan had been preoccupied with other things.

Namely, women and poetry.

Dan realized he didn't even know where Zeke had applied to college. The distance between them was mostly his fault, and he felt bad about it. "Hey Zeke," he called over.

Zeke stopped walking, his heavy body looking even more massive than usual inside his new parka. "Hey Dan," he replied with a careful smile, bouncing the blue ball in place on the frozen sidewalk. "Hey Vanessa."

"What do you think of Dan's new haircut?" Vanessa asked

with a wry smile. "It's part of his new Mr. Published Poet image."

"Oh yeah?" Zeke didn't seem to know what Vanessa was talking about. He glanced down the street, giving the basketball a good hard bounce before holding up his hand. "See you guys."

"See ya," Dan called, watching his old friend dribble the ball down to the end of the street.

"So, what's the big news?" Vanessa asked as they started to walk west on Seventy-eighth Street.

Cold air blasted the clouds across the pale gray sky. Down the block, through the leafless branches of the trees in Riverside Park, Dan caught a silvery glimpse of the Hudson. "Well," he began suspensefully. "This morning this big-deal literary agent named Rusty Klein called my cell phone and left me this crazy message. She thinks I'm the next Keats and she said we have to keep the momentum going now that we have the public's attention."

"Wow. Even *I've* heard of her!" Vanessa responded, impressed. "What does that mean, though?"

Dan blew a puff of smoke into the air. "I guess it means she wants to represent me."

Vanessa stopped walking. She wasn't sure where they were going anyway. "But you only wrote one poem. What's she going to do? I don't mean to be a downer Dan, but you have to be careful of people like that, you know? She could be trying to take advantage of you."

Dan stopped walking, too. He flipped up the collar of his black wool army-navy coat and then flipped it down again. Why was Vanessa being so negative? All of this was totally unexpected, but it was also extremely fucking cool. And it wasn't like he was going to sell out and start writing clichéd

Gap ads just because he had an agent, if that was what she was worried about. "I don't know. I think she can help me with my career. Maybe I can put a book together and she can try to get it published or something."

Vanessa blew on her hands and then rubbed her cold, bare ears. "Can we go over to your house? I'm freezing my ass off. We'd better work on the film, too."

Dan threw his cigarette on the ground. "Um, actually, I was thinking I might go back and read through all my notebooks. You know, see if there's a thematic link to some of the poems. Something I could work into a book."

Vanessa had been about to offer her services as a reader, but it didn't sound like Dan wanted any help. "Okay," she said coolly. "Call me if you need anything or whatever."

Dan flipped his collar up again and lit another cigarette, experimenting with his new look. "Oh, wait. I wanted to ask you something. Rusty Klein invited me to this thing called Better Than Naked. 'The Better Than Naked show.' That's what she said. Do you know if that's a band or something?"

Better Than Naked was the antifashion fashion label that Vanessa's older sister, Ruby, blew all her gig money on. Most of their clothes looked like old thrift-store rags that had been run over by a fleet of street-cleaning machines, which was completely intentional. Very downtown "fuck the trends" fashion.

"It's Fashion Week starting on Friday," Vanessa explained. "It sounds like she's inviting you to the Better Than Naked runway show, which I only know about because Ruby is totally crazy about their clothes and always watches the shows on the Metro Channel. I don't know why Rusty Klein thinks *you* would want to go, though. What do you care about clothes? And it'll be full of posers and wanna-bes—you know, that whole vapid fashion scene."

Dan looked thoughtful as he puffed on his cigarette. "I think I'm gonna check it out." He wouldn't have cared if Rusty Klein had asked to meet him at a pro wrestling match. This was about building his writing career.

Filming Dan at the Better Than Naked show would have been perfect material for her film, but Vanessa didn't want to butt in if Dan was meeting someone as important as Rusty Klein at the show. "Okay, Mr. Hot Shit Poet. Don't forget your old friends when you're driving around in a limo drinking champagne with naked models and whatnot." She reached up and mussed his neat little haircut. "Congratulations."

Dan grinned widely back at her. "It's pretty amazing," he agreed happily. Then, with one last sweet kiss, he turned and walked up Riverside Drive toward home, the iridescent silver Puma logos flashing on his heels as he went.

Vanessa smiled fondly at the spring in his step. "See you later, alligator."

s has just what they've been looking for

"I'm looking for one of those groovy new men's golfing jackets in a funky Day-Glo color like bright green or yellow," Serena told the salesgirl in the Les Best boutique on Tuesday after school. During French that day Serena had remembered admiring the new Les Best men's golfing jacket in the latest issue of *W* magazine and decided it was the perfect gift for Aaron. She never got tired of giving Aaron gifts. Everything she bought just looked so cute on him. It was like dressing a doll, her own adorable life-sized, dreadlocked, guitar-playing, Harvard-bound doll.

The boutique was on West Fourteenth Street in the meatpacking district, where the streets actually smelled like carcasses and manure from all the old meat warehouses. Leave it to Les Best, creator of the most beautifully tailored leisure wear in the world, to think that the rawness of the neighborhood was so cool, he just had to open up shop there. The space was huge and decorated all in white muslin with only one or two brightly colored tennis dresses or polo jackets hanging from giant steel hooks sticking out of the walls. The idea was that unless you really knew enough about the clothes to ask to see more, you had no purpose shopping there.

"We're all out of the golfing jackets, I'm afraid," the bleached-blond salesgirl answered in an English accent. She was dressed all in white, too. Even her sneakers were made of white pony fur. "My manager nicked the last one for himself."

Serena examined a gorgeous red-and-white-striped silk tennis dress hanging on a hook nearby. "Damn," she said under her breath. "I keep seeing that jacket in magazines and I thought it would be the perfect thing." Les Best was her favorite new designer, but maybe the clothes were a little too haute couture for Aaron anyway. He was more of a skater-boy kind of dresser. She hitched her deep gold leather Longchamp bag onto her shoulder. "Thanks for your help," she called, hoping to make it over to XLarge—a skate store on Lafayette Street—before it closed.

"Wait!" someone called out.

Serena paused in the doorway and turned around. Were they talking to her?

A tanned guy with a bleached-blond crew cut wearing the exact bright green golfing jacket she'd been hoping to buy for Aaron was holding open a white door in the back of the store. He smiled as he walked toward her. "I hope you don't mind my asking." He cocked his head and gave Serena the once-over. "Les asked me to look for a 'real girl' for his show in Bryant Park on Friday. I only caught a glimpse of you as you were leaving, but I just *know* you'd be perfect. I've seen your picture in the society pages. You're Serena, right?"

Serena nodded, unfazed. She was used to being recognized from photographs in gossip columns. She'd even had an unnamed body part photographed by the famous Remi brothers in October. The photo had been picked up by a New York Transit Authority arts project and had wound up being pasted all over the city.

"Are you interested?" the guy asked, raising his blond-tinted eyebrows hopefully. "You're just what we've been looking for."

Serena fiddled with the ties on her white cashmere earflap hat. This Friday she and Aaron had planned to spend the whole night together, drinking at Soap on the Lower East Side, watching late-night TV in her bedroom, and . . . hanging out.

Whatever *that* means.

Yes, I am *interested,* Serena thought. She and Aaron could hang out any time. They had the rest of their lives to hang out together! Getting asked to be in Les Best's show during New York Fashion Week was a once-in-a-lifetime opportunity. It wasn't like she wanted to make a career of modeling or anything, but this was her chance to show Les Best how much she truly appreciated his clothes. Plus, it would be *fun.* Aaron would understand that. In fact, he was such a wonderful boyfriend, he'd probably *encourage* her to do it.

"I'd love to," Serena answered finally. She pursed her not-too-full, not-too-thin lips and then grinned at her own ballsiness. "But only if I can have your jacket. I was looking for that exact one for my boyfriend and a little bird told me you took the last one."

"Oh my God, totally." The blond guy whipped off the bright green jacket and folded it expertly. Walking over to the register, he wrapped the jacket in black tissue paper and tucked it into a prized white Les Best shopping bag. "There you are, darling." He offered the bag to Serena. "I've only worn it for like, an hour. And it's on us, gratis. So, we'll see you in Les's tent in Bryant Park on Friday at 4 P.M. sharp, okay? You'll be on the list and you can invite four friends. Look for the girls holding clipboards and wearing headsets. They'll tell you exactly where to go."

Serena took the bag. *Score!*

"Don't I need to be fitted for anything, or practice walking on the runway, or whatever?" she asked, pulling her white cashmere cap down over her ears.

The guy rolled his eyes in a camp, don't-be-silly way. "Honey, you're a natural. Trust me, you'll look good no matter *what* you do." He handed her his card. *Guy Reed, Chief d'Affairs, Les Best Couture,* it read. "If you have any questions, just call." He gave her a quick kiss on the cheek. "Hey, what *is* that scent you're wearing?"

Serena smiled. She was used to people asking about her scent, too. "I mix it myself," she told him, fully aware that her answer was just as mysterious as the scent.

Guy closed his eyes and inhaled deeply. "Mmm. Dee-*lish*." He opened his eyes again. "I'm going to have to tell Les about that, too. He's been searching for a signature scent." He reached up and gave Serena's hat strings a playful tug with his tanned fingers. "See you Friday, doll. Stay warm. And don't forget, the after-party is even better than the show!"

Serena gave him a quick air kiss and then headed out into the cold. She couldn't wait to give Aaron his present and tell him the news. He could wear the jacket to the show and then they could drop by the after-party together so she could show him off.

Outside, she no sooner lifted her cashmere-mittened hand than four cabs on West Fourteenth Street screeched to a halt and honked for her attention.

See how difficult it is to be so beautiful?

v rocks people's worlds

Ruby was on another Martha Stewart spree, and the tantaliz-
ing scent of freshly baked brownies wafted into Vanessa's bedroom as she sorted through submissions for *Rancor*, the
Constance Billard student-run arts magazine of which she
was editor-in-chief. Heat blasted from the steaming radiators,
and the sounds of ambulance sirens and car horns wailed
through the two open windows. Vanessa's bare wooden floor
was scattered with the usual *Rancor* submissions: twenty
black-and-white photographs of clouds, feet, eyes, or the family dog; three short stories about learning to drive and feeling
the tug of independence despite the writer's appreciation for
her parents and all they'd done for her; and seven poems discussing the meaning of friendship.

Boring.

After the third short story, Vanessa retrieved Ruby's sugaring kit from the bathroom. Sugaring was an extremely messy,
all-natural, and "virtually painless" way of removing the hair
on your legs. You covered your legs with sticky brown goo,
applied a strip of white cloth, and then ripped the strip of
cloth away from your leg, taking the hair with it.

Painless? *Yeah, right.*

Vanessa kicked her black leggings onto the floor, laid a black bath towel over her black-and-gray patchwork bedspread, and sat down on top of it. She basted her pale, stocky calves with the sugary stuff, feeling like a giant glazed donut. Usually she was extremely low-maintenance, but if Dan was going to be hanging out with supermodels and agents and fashion designers, she thought she should at least try to make an effort and do something about the hair on her legs. Besides, spring was just around the corner. She might even go crazy and try sporting a miniskirt.

"Fuck!" she yelped, ripping off the first strip of gauze. Who'd come up with the idea that women were supposed to be all smooth and hairless like babies? What the hell was wrong with a little hair? Most men were covered with it.

She ripped off another strip. "Christ!" Okay, this was officially insane. Her skin was so raw and red she wouldn't have been surprised to see blood gushing from the hair follicles.

Her phone rang and she snatched it up and growled into it, "If this is you, Dan, I want you to know that I'm frigging ripping the hair off my body with my bare hands right now, and I'm doing it all for you, which is pretty fucking poetic if you ask me!"

"Hello? Vanessa Abrams? This is Ken Mogul, filmmaker. You sent me your New York film essay a few weeks ago. We met in the park on New Year's Eve?"

Vanessa sat up straight and adjusted the phone against her ear. Ken Mogul was only, like, one of the most famous alternative film directors ever. At Christmastime he'd happened upon a clip of Vanessa's work on the Web and had been so impressed he'd flown all the way from California to look her up. The problem was, he'd found her at exactly midnight on New Year's Eve, which had been exactly the same moment

Dan had shown up to give her a big fat New Year's Eve kiss. Needless to say, Vanessa had sort of blown Ken Mogul off, although she had made the effort to send him her New York film essay when it was finished.

"Yes, I remember," she answered quickly, completely amazed that the director even wanted to speak to her again. "What's up?"

"Well, I hope you don't mind, but I showed your film to Jedediah Angel, who's a personal friend of mine, and he wants to use it as a backdrop for his Fashion Week show this weekend."

Vanessa wrapped the black bath towel around her legs. It was sort of embarrassing talking to Ken Mogul when she was practically naked and covered in sugary brown goo. "Jeremiah what?" she asked. Ken always seemed to speak in Hollywoodese, and this time she had absolutely no clue what he was talking about.

"Jedediah Angel. He's a fashion designer. His label is called Cult of Humanity by Jedediah Angel? Very hot. Jed says you're the next Bertolucci. Your film's like the anti–*La Dolce Vita*. You really rocked his world."

Vanessa grinned. Why did people have to sound so cheesy just because they'd made it? She'd rocked his world? "Great," she replied, unsure of what to say. "Is there anything you need me to do?"

"Just come to the show and enjoy. I'll be there of course, and there are some people I want you to meet. You're already a moviemaking goddess, babe. You totally rock."

"Cool," Vanessa replied, slightly appalled that he'd actually told her she rocked not once but *twice*. "So what's the designer's name again?"

"Cult of Humanity by Jedediah Angel," Ken repeated

slowly. "Six P.M. Friday at Highway 1. It's a club in Chelsea."

"I've heard of it." It was the type of place Vanessa normally avoided like the plague. "I guess I'll see you there."

"Fan-fucking-tastic!" Ken enthused. "Ciao!"

Vanessa hung up and rubbed at a glop of dried sugaring paste on her wrist. Then she picked up the phone and dialed Dan's number without even looking at the keypad.

"Hello?" Jenny answered on the first ring.

"Hey Jennifer, it's Vanessa." Vanessa always called Jenny Jennifer because Jenny had asked her to.

"I'm not sure if Dan will talk to you. He wouldn't talk to *me*, and he's been locked in his room ever since he got home. It's so gross—there's cigarette smoke, like, *pouring* out from under the door."

Vanessa laughed and flopped back on her black pillows. Everything in her room was black, except the walls, which were dark red. "How do you know he's not in there putting gel in his hair? That new haircut looks pretty high maintenance."

The two girls snickered.

"I'll go see if I can get him. Hold on."

"What's up?" Dan picked up the phone a minute or two later. He sounded distracted. "Jenny said it was an emergency."

Vanessa lifted her leg in the air and tugged at another sugaring strip. It appeared to be glued permanently to her skin. Talk about emergencies!

"I thought you'd want to know that Ken Mogul just called. He said some designer named Jedediah Angel who has this fashion label called Culture of Humanitarianism or something is using my film essay as a backdrop for his fashion show on Friday night. Ken said I really 'rocked' Jedediah Angel's world." She snorted. "Isn't that hilarious?"

"That's *fantastic*," Dan responded earnestly. "Seriously. Congratulations."

Fantastic? Since when did Daniel Humphrey use words like *fantastic?* Vanessa didn't know what to say. Dan hadn't caught the sarcasm in her voice at all. As if she'd only called him to gloat about her success.

"Okay," she said evenly. "I just thought you'd want to know. I'll let you get back to work now." She thought of cracking a joke about how one day when they were both rich and famous they could buy big-ass mansions next door to each other in Beverly Hills. But then she decided against it. Dan would probably think she was serious. "Call me later if you feel like it, okay?"

"Okay," Dan replied, obviously distracted by whatever new poem he was working on.

After hanging up, Vanessa scooted off the bed. A corner of the black towel was now glued to the back of her left knee. She waddled into the bathroom to try and shower off the sugaring crap. Maybe one day when she was disgustingly rich and famous she'd have her own personal waxing and sugaring staff, but for now she'd have to get rid of the rest of the hair on her legs the old-fashioned way—with a pink plastic Daisy shaver.

gossipgirl.net

hey people!

The flavor-of-the-month club

So what ever became of that fake-breasted fake blond pop princess with the permanently bare midriff whose songs were *always* on the radio when you woke up in the morning and stayed in your head *all day*, driving you *insane*. I'll call her "Sally" here, so as not to offend any of her adoring fans, but I'm sure you know who I'm talking about. I heard she had a nervous breakdown and has been in rehab in Palm Springs ever since. She likes it so much there she's buying a ranch right next door, redoing it in shades of pink, and calling it Sallyland. If we're lucky, she'll stay there forever, only busting out in her late sixties to do overproduced cabaret shows on the Vegas Strip to prove that she can still lip-sync with the best of them despite her advanced age and drug-addled mind.

What about our favorite twenty-something actress who got into that bit of trouble with the law—something to do with carrying shopping bags full of items that didn't exactly belong to her out of a well-known department store? She's in rehab, too, but don't worry—the film industry will find a way to bring her back. In fact, that's what distinguishes the flavors of the month from the real stars. We kind of *want* to see her again. We want to know that there's life after being busted. We want to see her rise to new heights, whereas we don't much care what happens to Sally. At nineteen, she was already tired.

The ins and outs of rehab

Rehab and college are actually very similar as far as status is concerned. There are the select few, which are filled with celebrities and the children of the very rich, and then there are the rest of them, which are filled with regular people. Getting into the best ones is highly competitive, but once you're in, you're *in*. So I wouldn't worry about our darling **N**. He may be in trouble, but his parents aren't about to send him to the rehab equivalent of community college.

Your e-mail

Dear GG,
I'm an intern at Les Best Couture, and I heard Les sent a spy to **S**'s school to check out what she looked like. He was kind of mad that she was hired without him even seeing her.
—lilintern

Dear lil,
I bet he's not mad anymore though, right?
—GG

dear gossip girl,
how come you never mention **K** and **I** anymore? It makes me wonder if maybe you are one of them.
—eyespy

Dear eyespy,
I'll never tell, so wonder away!
—GG

Sightings

K and **I**—there, I mentioned them—in **Bryant Park**, freezing their butts off in skimpy **Blue Cult** denim miniskirts as they tried to get the interns working the doors of the **Fashion Week** tents to give them first- or second-row seats for Friday and Saturday's runway shows instead of their usual ones toward the back. **B** renting *How to Steal a Million*, starring **Audrey Hepburn**, for the seventeenth time at **Blockbuster** on Seventy-second and Lex. I guess that's *one* way of preparing for your **Yale** alum interview. **N** headed up the Merritt Parkway toward Connecticut in the back seat of his parents' black **Mercedes SUV**. On his way to rehab, maybe? **V** in **Barneys**, of all places, checking out a frayed black hemp driving coat with chain-mail seams and vintage hook-and-eye buttons by **Culture of Humanity by Jedediah Angel**. She looked tempted, but at that price she'd be better off ripping up her own clothes and fastening them together with paper clips.

My problem isn't getting into the first row—it's which show to go to. They *all* want me! Sigh. Being popular can be seriously hard work.

You know you love me.

gossip girl

j and *e* explore their problem areas

"Five more minutes, ladies," announced Ms. Crumb to her Constance Billard ninth-grade creative writing class. She pulled her curly black hair out of the way and prodded the wax in her right ear with the eraser of a yellow number two pencil. "Remember, it's not *what* you're writing about but *how* you describe it."

None of the girls looked up. They were too busy writing, and besides, they really didn't want to see what Ms. Crumb was doing when she thought they weren't looking. They'd already been grossed out enough times.

According to the girls, *all* the female teachers at Constance Billard were lesbians, but Ms. Crumb was the only teacher at Constance who was officially out. She wore a rainbow pin to school every day, shared a country house in New Paltz with five other women, and often referred to her "partner"—as in, "The other night my partner was drinking Amstel Lite and watching Barbara Walters, who she has a total crush on, while I sat in the kitchen and graded your papers." Every year the ninth graders looked forward to having Ms. Crumb's creative writing class, assuming she'd be cool and down-to-earth since she was so forthright about her sexuality. But after a day in her classroom her students realized they weren't just going to sit around for forty-five minutes talking about girl stuff with a woman who liked girls—they were going to have to write things every day in class, read them out loud, and then listen to Ms. Crumb and their classmates criticize what they had written in a sometimes not very nice way. Ms. Crumb was a major hardass, but as far as subjects went, creative writing was still a hell of a lot better than geometry.

Today Ms. Crumb had asked the girls to pick a partner—in the platonic sense—and write a paragraph describing a part of their partner's body. Of course Elise and Jenny had picked each other. They were beginning to do almost everything together.

It's odd that we decorate our ears with earrings and don't try to cover them, Jenny wrote. *They're just as indecent as the parts we do cover, like bare holes that go straight into our heads. My friend Elise's ears are small, with a little blond fuzz on them. She has good hearing, too, because she never says, "What?" and asks me to repeat myself. I guess she keeps them pretty clean.*

Jenny looked up and decided to erase the last line and replace it with something else. Ms. Crumb might get offended, since she obviously had some kind of ear-cleaning fetish.

But instead of writing something else to replace the ear-cleaning line, Jenny's mind wandered back to her e-mail. She'd been checking it regularly, just like Blair had told her to; however, the only messages she'd gotten had been jokey ones from Elise and her brother, telling her to stop checking her e-mail and get back to her homework. She glanced at Elise, who was scribbling away, already on her second page. Jenny wished she had Dan's knack for the written word. She was better at detailed drawings and painting and calligraphy.

At the top of the page she drew an elaborate drawing of Elise's ear and the side of her face, hoping she'd score points for being artistic, even if her essay sucked. Her mind wandered again, to the blond boy she'd spotted in Bendel's. Was he artistic, too?

The bell rang to mark the end of last period and Ms. Crumb stood up and brushed chalk dust from her dark gray wool pinafore dress that looked like it had been made by nuns somewhere cold and fashionless, like Greenland.

"Time's up, ladies. Pencils down. You can hand in your papers as you leave." She tucked her maroon-stockinged feet into a pair of black felt L.L. Bean clogs. "Happy Thursday afternoon!"

"So what'd you write about?" Jenny asked Elise after they had packed up their book bags and were on their way out the school doors.

"None of your business," Elise answered, blushing.

"Don't think I'm never going to find out. You'll probably have to read it out loud on Monday," Jenny reminded her. "I wrote about your ears, but it kind of sucked."

The two girls bowed their heads against the fierce February wind and headed over to Lexington to take the bus down to Bloomingdale's on East Fifty-ninth Street. Elise had enlisted Jenny to help her to find the perfect pair of jeans for less than eighty dollars, and, as usual, Jenny needed some new bras, since she was always wearing out the elastic or breaking the underwires in the ones she had.

Bloomingdale's was a tacky war zone of tourists sporting the new tracksuits and sneakers they'd just bought at Nike Town, along with gaggles of blue-haired bargain hunters, but it was the only place to go for oversized bras and moderately priced jeans other than Macy's, which was simply gross.

Those with better taste and bigger credit limits went to Bergdorf's, Bendel's, or Barneys, but for people like Jenny and Elise, Bloomingdale's would just have to do.

"I can't believe you can just put those on and they're the perfect length," Jenny said enviously as she watched Elise try on her first pair of Paris Blues jeans in the dressing room. Jenny was barely five feet tall and had to shorten everything. Elise was five foot seven, but she had other problems, like her completely flat chest and the podge that padded her hip bones and lower back like a second butt.

Elise scrunched up her freckled face and stared down at the bulges riding above the waistband of the low rise jeans. "See why I can't eat in public?" she grunted, sucking in her stomach and tugging on the waistband. The jeans were 9 percent Lycra, but that didn't seem to make much difference. She exhaled and let her stomach out, giving up. "Okay, forget it. Next pair."

As Elise inched herself out of the reject ones, Jenny held up a beautiful pair of dark rinse flared Seven jeans that were on sale and would be a major score if they fit. She noticed Elise was wearing light blue lacy underwear and quickly averted her eyes so Elise wouldn't accuse her of staring.

Elise took the jeans, slipped her feet into them and slid them up around her hips. "Oh my God. I can't believe I forgot to tell you this," she said, tugging on the button-fly waist. "Before creative writing I heard Kati Farkas and Isabel Coates talking about Nate Archibald in the bathroom at school. They said he almost had to go to *jail* because he was caught dealing to some twelve-year-olds in the park. His dad had to go down to the police station and bail him out, but he still has to go to *rehab*. Weren't you guys kind of *together* for a little while? Did you hear about this? Isn't it crazy?"

Jenny hadn't heard, and she wasn't quite sure how she felt about it. Nate had pretty much blown her off completely in the end, brushing her away like a pesky fly, so she guessed he'd gotten what he deserved. Besides, Nate seemed like the type of guy who would always rise to the top again, unscathed. Why should she waste any more time worrying or even *thinking* about him? She watched Elise struggle with the copper buttons on her jeans. They were perfect everywhere else, but the waist was so tight there was no way she'd ever be able to sit down in them. "Why don't you just try the next size up?"

Elise squinted her hard blue eyes stubbornly. She did that kind of a lot, causing Jenny to wonder if she needed glasses. "Because, Miss Size Zero, I'm a size seven, not a size nine. Pass me another pair, and stop staring at my fat."

"I'm not," Jenny insisted, handing her a stretchy pair of Lei jeans that were a little too distressed, with frayed cuffs and holes in the pockets, but with a wide, low waist that looked like it might actually sit nicely on Elise's hips. "And it's not like anyone has to know what size you are. I won't tell." Jenny immediately thought of her own size issue. She hadn't planned on inviting Elise into the dressing room with her when she tried on bras. Sure, they were becoming close friends, but was it really necessary for Elise to know that she wasn't just a D cup, but a *double* D? Still, it seemed mean not to reciprocate when Elise had invited her to help try on jeans.

Elise wrinkled up her nose at the Leis. "Those are way too fake looking."

"So what do you want to do?" Jenny asked, tossing the jeans on the bench in the back of the narrow dressing room.

Elise buttoned up her uniform and slid her feet into her prissy black flats. It amazed Jenny how neat-and-sweet-little-school-girl Elise appeared until you got to know her.

"I'm keeping the Sevens. I know they don't fit now, but I'm planning to lose ten pounds before the end of the year. And *you're* going to help me."

Jenny nodded. It wasn't like she didn't ever buy stuff that was too small.

Yes, it's called *aspirational* shopping. Every girl with ambition does it.

The dressing rooms in the lingerie department were dirty, cramped, and badly lit. With her back to Elise, Jenny pulled her cornflower blue V-neck J. Crew sweater over her head and threw it on the stool in the corner. Then she pulled her white Gap T-shirt off and dropped it on the floor, crossing her arms over her breasts self-consciously.

"Which one do you want to try on first?" Elise asked, sorting through the plastic hangers that Jenny had hastily snatched up with businesslike efficiency. "The lacy black one with the funky clasp or the comfy white cotton one with the extrawide straps?"

"Just hand me the black one," Jenny mumbled, reaching behind her to retrieve the bra. She unhooked the ugly beige supersupportive Bali bra she was wearing and let it fall to the floor, fumbling with the black bra while trying to keep the insides of her elbows pressed against her ribcage to cover herself. The straps on the black bra were shortened all the way, and the clasp was a strange gold metal contraption instead of the normal hook and eye. Jenny glanced up to find Elise watching her in the mirror. The dressing room had mirrors on three sides, so it wasn't like Jenny was really achieving anything by turning her back.

"Want some help?" Elise took a step forward.

Jenny's back was rigid. She could pretty much forget about being modest. Elise was going to see her boobs no matter what. She let her arms drop and turned around, full frontal. "Help me loosen the straps?" she asked, trying to sound nonchalant. She handed Elise the bra, her breasts hanging in front of her like fully risen loaves of sourdough bread. She had to admit it felt slightly liberating. Slightly liberating and totally embarrassing.

Elise set to work adjusting the bra, not even trying to hide the fact that she was staring at Jenny's boobs at the same time. "Wow. They really *are* big," she observed. "How can you be so tiny and have such big bobos?"

Jenny put her hands on her hips and stared back at Elise, trying to come up with a smart retort, but instead she burst out laughing. "Bobos?" she giggled.

Elise blushed and handed Jenny back the bra. "I've always called them that. Ever since I was little."

Jenny slid the straps over her arms and then turned around. "Can you figure out the clasp?" Elise hooked it closed and Jenny turned around again. The bra had great support, but her boobs were pressed so close together, her cleavage was a mile deep. Elise was still staring. "Do you think it's too slutty?" Jenny asked. She giggled. "I mean, this kind of makes my bobos look even bigger."

Elise had stopped blinking, which was what she always did when she was distracted. "You know when you asked me what I wrote about today in creative writing?" she asked. Jenny nodded and turned around so Elise could unhook the bra. "Well, that's what I wrote about. Your bobos."

Jenny's back went rigid again. If a guy told you he'd written about your breasts, you pretty much knew he was either hitting on you or he was a pervert. But since Elise was a girl and her friend, Jenny wasn't sure how to feel about it.

"I think I'm done," she said quickly. She picked her old

bra up off the floor and slipped it on. "I'm going to buy the black one."

They'd brought eight bras into the dressing room but Jenny had only tried on one. "Are you sure you don't want to try some of the others?" Elise asked.

Jenny pulled on her T-shirt and tucked her sweater under her arm. The tiny dressing room suddenly felt extremely claustrophobic. "Nah," she answered, yanking aside the black curtain and stepping back into the main room of the lingerie department, which of course was wall-to-wall bras. It would be nice to go someplace where breasts weren't the main focus of everyone's attention.

Like another planet?

b has hots for older man

"Would you like another Coke, miss?" the bow-tied cocktail server asked.

"No, thank you," Blair answered, keeping her eyes glued to the door.

All week long her mind had been on one thing only: her interview with Owen Wells. She had even done some research on the Internet so she could ask him pointed questions about Wells, Trachtman, & Rice, the law firm where he was a partner. Now it was finally Thursday night and she was sitting alone at the corner table in Leneman's Bar in the Compton Hotel, waiting for him. The bar was crowded, mostly with middle-aged men in custom-tailored suits, discussing business deals over bourbon on the rocks, or sitting with bleached-blond women who were very definitely not their wives. With its golden walls, crisp white tablecloths, and forties jazz music, the bar had an air of sexy sophistication.

Blair had spent almost three hours getting ready: one to shower and blow her hair out into a neat, preppy coif that framed her face in an innocent yet intellectual manner; one to dress in her new belted Les Best jersey dress, which she had paired with her lucky pair of three-inch Ferragamo heels, to give her an extra bit of confidence and height; and one to apply natural-looking makeup for the fresh, healthy glow of someone who always got twelve hours of sleep because she never went out and never went near a cigarette or a cocktail.

Right.

It was still only a quarter to nine, but if she drank any more Coke, she'd have to pee so badly she'd never make it through the interview without wetting herself. What Blair really wanted was a shot of Stoli, but with her luck Owen Wells would stroll through the door just as she was knocking back the shot, confirming his worries that she really was just a flaky party girl who only wanted to go to Yale to get drunk and seduce the captain of the crew team, possibly getting pregnant in the process and forcing that innocent, previously upstanding Yale male to marry her and work like a slave for the rest of his life to keep her in the style she was accustomed to.

Just then an extremely well groomed businessman sitting at the bar spun around on his gold-painted barstool and smiled at her. He had wavy black hair, bright blue eyes with long curly lashes, and distinctly arched black eyebrows. His face and hands were deeply tanned, as if he played tennis in the sun every day of his life, and he was wearing a gorgeous navy blue wool suit with a crisp white shirt and simple gold cuff links. Blair didn't usually notice older guys, and this guy was at least thirty-eight, but he was so handsome, it was impossible *not* to notice.

"Are you Blair Waldorf, by any chance?" he asked in a deep, familiar voice.

Blair nodded tentatively. "Yes?"

He slid off his stool and walked over to her table, leaving an empty glass tumbler behind on the bar. He held out his right hand. "I'm Owen Wells."

"Hi!" Blair jumped to her feet and took his hand, feeling completely confused. First of all, Owen Wells was her father's colleague, so he should have been old, badly dressed, balding, and fat. Not that her father was. Her father worked out with a personal trainer every day, wore designer clothes, and had great hair. But he was *gay*. Second of all, Owen Wells had said he'd be wearing his Yale tie, and this guy wasn't wearing a tie at all, just a crisp white dress shirt, unbuttoned so she could see the top of the clean white undershirt he was wearing over his muscular chest, which was probably just as tan as the rest of him.

Not that she was thinking about *the rest of him*.

Third of all, she hadn't expected Owen Wells to be *hot*. He looked so much like Cary Grant in *An Affair to Remember* that she wanted to throw herself into his arms and tell him to forget about Yale, she was his, *all his*.

Blair came to her senses in time to realize that she was still grasping Owen's hand. She shook it as firmly and confidently as she could, alarmed by her mind's total inability to focus on the task at hand. She was meeting with Owen for one reason only: to impress him so she could get into Yale. "Thank you for taking the trouble to meet with me," she added hastily.

"I've been looking forward to it," he replied in his thrilling, manly voice. "I just remembered I told you I'd be wearing my Yale tie. Sorry. It completely slipped my mind. I even saw you come in, but I didn't think it could be you. I wasn't expecting you to be early."

Immediately Blair wondered if he'd noticed that she'd spent twenty minutes in the bathroom after she'd arrived, or that she'd kept wiping her nose on her cocktail napkin and studying her face in her Stila compact mirror to check for any unsightly blemishes, like a stray eye goober or—God forbid— a pimple.

"I'm usually early," she answered. "I'm never late." She took a nervous sip of Coke. Was this a good time to tell him how impressed she was with his work on the *Home Depot* vs. *The Learning Channel* case? Should she compliment his suit? She took a deep breath and tried to focus. "I like it here," she declared and immediately regretted it. It was a nice bar, but she made it sound like she wanted to move in or something.

Owen pulled back the chair opposite hers and gestured for her to sit down. "So, should we get started?"

Blair was grateful for his relaxed but businesslike manner. She sat down on the edge of the cushioned chair and crossed her legs primly. "Yes!" She beamed at him enthusiastically. "Whenever you're ready."

The cocktail waiter appeared to offer Owen another drink. He ordered a Maker's Mark and cocked a dark eyebrow at Blair. "Can I get you something besides a Coke? I promise I won't tell Yale or your dad."

Blair scrunched up her toes inside her black Ferragamos. If she said yes, she'd be admitting that she really did want a drink, and if she said no, she might seem like a prude. "I'll have a glass of chardonnay," she told him, figuring white wine was the safest, most ladylike option.

"So. Tell me why Yale should admit you," Owen asked after he'd ordered the wine. He leaned across the table and lowered his voice. "Are you really as bright as your dad claims?"

Blair sat up even straighter, twirling her little ruby ring around and around on her ring finger beneath the tablecloth. "I think I'm smart enough to go to Yale," she replied evenly, remembering her speech. "I'm in all the APs at school. I'm at the top of the class. I'm the chair of the social services board and the French club. I'm a peer group leader. I'm nationally ranked in tennis. And I ran the organizing committee for five charity events this past year."

Their drinks arrived and Owen raised his glass. "And why Yale?" He took a sip. "What can Yale do for you?"

It seemed odd that Owen wasn't taking notes or anything, but maybe he was testing her, trying to get her to let down her guard and admit that she really was just a flake who'd been born with a silver spoon up her well-bred ass and only wanted to go to Yale to party with frat boys.

"As you know, Yale has an excellent prelaw program," she stated, determined to give intelligent, straight-to-the-point answers. "I'm thinking of going into entertainment law."

"Excellent." Owen nodded approvingly. He scooted his chair forward and winked at her. "Look, Blair. You're an intelligent, ambitious girl. I already know you're perfect for Yale and I promise I'll do everything I can to convince them to let you in."

He looked so handsomely earnest while he was saying this that Blair felt her cheeks heat up. She took a sip of wine to cool herself off. "Thank you," she responded gratefully. She took another sip of wine and let out an enormous sigh of gratitude and relief. "Thank you. Thank you, thank you, thank you."

Just then a pair of cool hands covered her eyes and she smelled the distinctive patchouli-and-sandalwood scent of a certain someone's favorite essential oil mixture.

"Guess who!" Serena whispered in Blair's ear, then pulled her hands away from Blair's eyes, her long blond hair brushing Blair's shoulder as she kissed her cheek. "What's going on?"

Behind her, Aaron stood grinning goofily, wearing a maroon Harvard sweatshirt like the annoying asshole he was.

Blair blinked. Could they not see she was in the middle of the most important meeting of her life?

"I'm Serena." Serena held out her hand for Owen to shake.

Owen stood up and took her hand. "Charmed." He bowed his dark head, looking more like Cary Grant than ever.

"So you're coming to see me in the Les Best show tomorrow, right?" Serena asked Blair.

"You *have* to come," Aaron chimed in. "I ain't going to no fashion show by myself, girlfrien'." He'd agreed to go, but he wasn't exactly looking forward to it. Fashion meant fur and animal testing. It was against everything he stood for.

"Your name is on the list," Serena added.

Owen looked completely bemused by the whole conversation. Blair let out an exasperated breath and stood up, turning away from Owen so he couldn't hear what she said. "Do you guys mind leaving us alone?" she hissed in a low whisper. "We're talking about Yale, and it's pretty fucking *important*."

Aaron put his arm around Serena's slim waist, pulling her away. "Excuse us," he responded in a patronizing whisper, still looking smug in his retarded Harvard sweatshirt. "We're headed down to that new club on Harrison, in case you want to catch us later." They waltzed out of the bar, his dreadlocks bouncing and her pale gold hair fanned out over her shoulders, both looking so carefree and careless, it was infuriating.

"Sorry," Blair apologized, crossing her ankles daintily as she sat down again. "My friends can be pretty self-absorbed sometimes."

"That's all right." Owen stared down into his bourbon, looking pensive as he stirred the ice cubes around in his glass. He looked up again. "Do you mind my asking what you did in your first Yale interview that was so awful you think they're not going to let you in?"

Blair took another sip of her wine, and then another. As soon as she explained what had happened, Owen was going to change his mind about her for sure. "I was having a bad day," she confessed, the words tumbling out of her mouth as she frantically spun her ruby ring around and around on her finger. She didn't want to go into the gory details of her botched interview, but if Owen was going to help her, he'd best know the truth. "I hadn't gotten enough sleep. I was tired and nervous and I had to pee really badly. The interviewer said, 'Tell me about yourself,' and before I could really think about what I was saying, I told him all about how my dad was gay and my mom was going to marry this gross, fat, red-faced guy with an annoying teenage son with dreadlocks who you just had the pleasure of meeting. I told him my boyfriend, Nate, was ignoring me. Then he asked me what books I'd been reading lately and I couldn't think of the title of a single book. I started to cry, and then, at the end of the interview, I kissed him." Blair sighed dramatically, snatched her cocktail napkin off the table, and began to shred it in her lap. "It was only on the cheek, but it was still totally inappropriate. I just wanted him to remember me. You know, you only get a few minutes to make an impression, but I guess I went a little overboard." She looked up into Owen's sympathetic blue eyes. "I don't know what I was thinking."

Owen sipped his drink silently as he considered the information. "I'll see what I can do," he responded finally, but his voice sounded detached and skeptical now.

Blair swallowed. It was pretty obvious he thought she was hopelessly stupid and insane. Oh, God. She was *ruined*.

Suddenly he broke into a devilish white-toothed grin. "I'm only joking, Blair. That doesn't sound so bad. It was probably the most memorable, entertaining interview Jason Anderson III has ever had. Face it, he's not the most exciting guy in the world, and his job has got to be a little monotonous. I'm sure you were the highlight of the fall interview season."

"So you don't think it's hopeless after all?" Blair asked in her most tragic Audrey-needs-your-help voice.

Owen took her small, ruby-ringed hand in his large tanned one. "Not at all." He cleared his throat. "Has anyone ever told you you look a bit like Audrey Hepburn?"

Blair blushed from the roots of her hair down to her toenail cuticles. Owen seemed to know exactly the right things to say, and he looked so much like Cary Grant, it made her dizzy. His thick gold wedding ring pressed into the bones on the back of her hand. She frowned down at it. If he was so married, what was he doing holding her hand?

Owen withdrew his hands and shifted in his seat, reading her mind. "Yes, I'm married, but we're not together anymore."

Blair nodded hesitantly. It was really none of her business. Although if Cary—Owen—wanted to ask her out again, she wouldn't exactly say no.

Ask her out again? Was she forgetting this wasn't exactly a date?

"So, I'm sure you have to get back to your AP homework and all that." Owen reached for her hand again as if he couldn't bear to let her go. "But do you mind if I call you again sometime?"

Blair hoped she looked *exactly* like Audrey at this very moment. Yes, Owen was nearly her father's age, a lawyer, a *man*, but she'd never felt so strongly attracted to anyone in her life. Why fight it? It was her second semester of senior year. She'd worked hard throughout high school and was hopefully getting into Yale soon. Yes, seeing an older man was crazy and irresponsible, but it was about time she had a little fun.

"Sure." She smiled and cocked her neatly plucked right eyebrow theatrically. "I'd like that."

gossipgirl.net

Disclaimer: All the real names of places, people, and events have been altered or abbreviated to protect the innocent. Namely, me.

hey people!

Teen heiress sells horses for drugs!

Last night I was out at that new club on Harrison, and between sips of the club's signature "adult" version of the Shirley Temple I got the latest scoop on one of my nursery-school classmates. Although she's heir to the largest lumber fortune in the entire world, she was recently caught selling her show horses for drug money. Apparently she doesn't come into her inheritance until she's eighteen and only gets a "small" monthly allowance. She was short on cash, so she took Guns'n'Roses, her prized show jumper, down to auction and used the money to buy some speed or whatever she does. How tacky is that? Apparently her eighty-year-old nanny—or whoever looks after her now that her father has passed away and her mother has moved to Sandy Lane in Barbados—found out about the horse and sent my old friend straight to rehab.

Sounds like rehab is the place to be this winter!

Fashion Week: the lowdown

Expect to freeze your ass off while trying to hail a cab. Expect to wait an hour for a show to start only to be told that the show is running *another* hour late. Expect to see lots of Botoxed, fake-tanned, anorexic girls trying not notice that they all wore the same thing to the same show, and lots of gay men wearing more perfume than the girls. Expect to find out that those ugly-ass cargo pants with tapered legs are back in style *again*. Expect to be envious of the pouty-lipped, giraffe-legged models who actually look good in them. Expect to be annoyed by heavily made-up, fur-wearing women who bring their little Louis Vuitton collar–wearing French bulldogs to the show in matching Louis Vuitton handbags. Expect to be dying for the after-party to start so you can smoke. Expect the after-parties to be truly mind-blowing. Expect not to remember what happened the morning after.

Your e-mail

Dear GG,
I was walking by the bar in the Compton Hotel last night and I saw B with this man who I recognize from my building. He has a daughter who's like in ninth or tenth grade at my school. What's that all about?
—Tom

Hey Tom,
Who knows what she was up to, but can't you totally see B as some poor girl's evil stepmom?
—GG

Dear G-Dawg,
Can I just say that you kick ass! Also, I heard N is going to that fancy rehab up in Greenwich. My cousin went there and came back more messed up than before.
—F.B.

Dear F.B.,
Thanks for the compliment, although I don't know if I dig the whole "G-Dawg" thing. And whatever happens to N in rehab, they can't take away his soul or his divine beauty!
 GG

Sightings

N and his parents having a tour of that stylin' new rehab clinic in **Greenwich**. **C** having his nails done at **Coin**, an all-male spa in Chelsea. No kidding. **S** picking up a custom-made baby tee at one of those customized T-shirt places in **Chinatown**. **B** standing in front of **Tiffany**, drinking out of a paper cup and eating a Danish, just like

Audrey Hepburn in *Breakfast at Tiffany's,* except **B** was wearing her gray school uniform instead of a black **Christian Dior** evening gown. **K** and **I** putting up No Loitering signs around the **Les Best** tent. It looks like they actually *volunteered* their services so they could get good seats.

It's supposed to snow like crazy this weekend but has that ever stopped us? See you in the front row!

You know you love me.

gossip girl

kindred spirits connect in rehab

"Has everyone heard about the snowstorm? We're supposed to get four feet by midnight!" Jackie Davis, Nate's teen group facilitator at the Breakaway Rehabilitation Center, rubbed her hands together as if the idea of being snowed in with all these rich derelicts was her idea of a rocking good time.

After Nate had gotten busted in the park, his father and Saul Burns, the family lawyer, had come to fetch him at the precinct. Nate's father, a stern, silver-haired navy captain who handled emergencies with crisp, efficient formality, had paid the fine of three thousand dollars and cosigned an agreement that Nate would immediately attend a drug rehabilitation program for a minimum of ten hours per week. That meant Nate was going to have to ride the train out to Greenwich, Connecticut, five days a week for counseling and group therapy.

"Just think of it as a job, son," Saul Burns had tried to reassure him. "An after-school job." Captain Archibald hadn't said anything. It was pretty clear that Nate had disappointed him beyond words. Luckily Nate's mother had been in Monte Carlo visiting her thrice-divorced sister. When Nate had relayed the sordid tale over the phone she'd shrieked and wept, smoked five cigarettes in rapid succession, and then broken her champagne glass. She was always a little dramatic. After all, she was French.

"All right. Let's start out by going around the circle," Jackie instructed in a sunny voice, as if this were the first day of nursery school. "Tell us your name and explain why you're here. Keep it short, please." She nodded at Nate to start, since he was sitting directly to her right.

Nate shifted uncomfortably in his Eames chair. All the furniture at the posh Greenwich, Connecticut, rehab clinic was twentieth-century modern, to match the minimalist beige and white décor. The floor was cream-colored Italian marble, crisp white linen curtains covered the floor-to-ceiling windows, and the staff wore beige linen uniforms designed especially by nineties denim impresario Gunner Gass, a former patient who was now on the facility's board.

"Okay. My name's Nathaniel Archibald, but everyone calls me Nate," Nate mumbled. He kicked at the legs of his chair and cleared his throat. "I got busted a few days ago buying weed in Central Park. That's why I'm here."

"Thank you, Nate," Jackie interrupted. She smiled a frosty, brown-lipsticked smile and made a note on the pad in her clipboard. "We prefer it here at Breakaway if you call the substance in question by its true name. In your case, marijuana. If you can use its name consistently, you are making one more step toward your freedom from it." She smiled at Nate once more. "Would you like to try again?"

Nate glanced self-consciously at the other losers in the group. There were seven of them altogether, three guys and four girls, all staring at the floor, worrying about what they were going to say and looking just as uncomfortable as he felt.

"I'm Nate," Nate repeated mechanically. "A narc caught me buying *marijuana* in the park. That's why I'm here." Across the circle a girl with dark brown hair that hung down almost to her waist, bloodred lips, and skin so pale it was almost blue gazed at him soulfully, like a coked-up version of Snow White.

"Better," Jackie said. "Next." She nodded at the Japanese girl sitting next to Nate.

"My name is Hannah Koto and I took Ecstasy before school two weeks ago and got caught because I laid down on the floor to feel the rug in my trig class."

Everybody laughed except for Jackie. "Thank you, Hannah, that was fine. Next."

Nate tuned the next two people out, kind of grooving on the way Snow White was jiggling her foot, like she was keeping time to her own private concert. She was wearing light blue suede boots that looked like they'd never been worn outside.

Suddenly it was her turn. "My name is Georgina Spark. Everyone calls me Georgie. I guess I'm here because I wasn't very nice to my father before he croaked, so I have to wait until I turn eighteen before I can live my life the way I want to."

The rest of the group tittered nervously. Jackie frowned. "Can you name the substance you were found abusing, Georgina?"

"Cocaine," Georgie answered, letting a curtain of dark hair fall over her face. "I sold my favorite show horse to buy fifty grams. It was in the papers and everything. *New York Post*, Thursday, February—"

"Thank you," Jackie interrupted. "Next group member please."

Still jiggling her foot, Georgie glanced up through her hair and met Nate's intrigued gaze with a mischievous bloodred smile.

"*Bitch*," she mouthed, obviously referring to Jackie.

Nate grinned back and nodded his chin ever so slightly. Saul Burns had told him to treat rehab like an after-school job. Now he had a reason to work hard at it.

s wears her love like a baby tee

"You're friends with that Serena chick, right?" Sonny Webster, a lanky boy with jet-black hair streaked with paper-bag-brown highlights asked Chuck Bass as they sat in the second row, waiting for the Les Best show to begin on Friday night. Sonny was the son of Vivienne Webster, a British lingerie designer whose hip-hugging boy shorts were all the rage at the moment. Sonny and Chuck had met in a bar last night and were already fast friends. They were even wearing matching Tods moccasins— dark brown with neon green rubber soles. Very gay urban yachtsman, and extremely impractical for the unprecedented amount of snow that had been predicted for that evening.

Chuck nodded. "She's appearing naked. That's what I heard, anyway." He rubbed his newly toned stomach. "I can't wait," he added halfheartedly.

"See Chuck talking to whatshisname, Vivienne Webster's totally gay son?" Kati Farkas whispered to Isabel Coates. "I swear Chuck's into guys now." She and Isabel had made it to the front row, just as they'd set out to do. Not because of their completely unnecessary little volunteer effort hanging up No Loitering signs around Bryant Park but because Isabel's father, Arthur Coates, was a very famous actor who'd complained that his daughter and her friend *deserved* to be in the front row this year because he'd already spent a fortune on Les Best's entire spring-summer collection.

"I think maybe he's bi," Isabel whispered back. "He's still wearing that gold monogrammed pinky ring."

"Yeah," noted Kati. "Like that's not totally gay."

The huge white tent in Bryant Park was packed with fashion magazine editors, photographers, actresses, and socialites. Blondie's "Heart of Glass" pounded out of Bose speakers. Christina Ricci sat in the front row on her cell phone arguing with her publicist and defending her decision to come to Les Best's show instead of Jedediah Angel's, which was happening downtown at exactly the same time.

"Look, there's Flow from 45!" Sonny squealed. "He's such a *god*. And there's Christina Ricci. My mom just got a huge order from her."

As Chuck gazed around the room, looking for more celebs and trying to be seen himself, he spotted Blair about ten seats down in the third row. He blew her a kiss and she smirked back.

"Why are we here again?" Blair yawned to Aaron. Even though she was completely annoyed with Serena these days, she'd decided to come to the show to see if any of Les Best's autumn collection suited her new image. Now that she was packed into the hot, crowded tent with its overly loud music and overwhelming perfume stench like a twelve-year-old with a general admission ticket at a 45 concert, she honestly couldn't give two fucks about the clothes or that Serena was the star of the show. It was all Serena needed to prove that she really was the center of the universe.

Blair didn't need to hang out with gorgeous models and camp fashion designers, anyway. She was going to Yale, the premier institution of higher learning in the entire world, *and* she was going to be asked out *very soon* by a classy older man. She felt extremely accomplished for someone so young. The noise and glitz of Fashion Week seemed less alluring now that her own life was so . . . *stimulating*. Plus they were seated in the third row, which was a major insult when she'd always been seated in the first or second row at every other show she'd ever been to.

"I'm honestly not sure why I'm here," Aaron answered grumpily. He unzipped the bright green Les Best golfing jacket Serena had given him and then zipped it up again. The jacket was made of stiff cotton canvas that made a loud, swishy sound when he moved. It was way too flashy for his taste, but he'd kept it on because Serena had insisted that he couldn't come to a fashion show and sit in the third row without wearing an article of the designer's clothing. Aaron liked the buzzy vibe of the fashion show. It was like being at a rock concert. But it was just so bogus that they were all gathered there to look at . . . *clothes*.

Outside the snow had been falling steadily on the brightly lit city for over two hours. Blair could just imagine how insane it was going to be to find a cab home later that night, with everyone totally underdressed, totally buzzed, and all thinking they deserved the next available ride. She kicked the back of Nicky Hilton's chair with her black patent leather Les Best flats and yawned for the fiftieth time. While her mouth was still stretched open in full yawn, the lights suddenly dimmed and the music stopped. The show was about to begin.

The collection being shown was for next fall, and the theme was Little Red Riding Hood. The stage was decorated like a fairy tale forest, with dark brown velvet tree trunks and low branches covered in glittering emerald green silk leaves. Fluttery flute music began to play, and suddenly Serena skipped onstage wearing her gray pleated Constance Billard

School uniform skirt, red suede over-the-knee boots, and a little red wool minicape tied at the neck. Under the cape she was wearing her own white baby tee with I LOVE AARON emblazoned in black across the chest. Her long blond hair was done in pigtails, and her face was free of makeup, except for her lips, which were painted a bright, thrilling red. Serena walked the runway with easy confidence, flouncing her pleated uniform skirt, twirling around, and then pausing for the cameras like she'd been doing it for years.

Who is she? A hundred gossip-starved voices murmured at once. *And who is Aaron?*

Blair rolled her eyes, even more bored and annoyed now that the show was under way.

"Who's Aaron?" Sonny whined to Chuck Bass.

"The fuck if I know," Chuck answered back.

"Is that supposed to be Aaron Sorkin? You know, the television writer?" a bewildered fur-wearing *Vogue* editor asked her neighbor.

"Whoever he is, he's one lucky dude," said a photographer.

"I heard he dumped her. I guess she's trying to win him back," Isabel snickered to Kati.

"Well, don't look now, but I think that's him, and he looks pissed," Kati hissed back. Both girls turned to stare.

Serena blew Aaron a kiss from the runway, but Aaron was too busy feeling hot and embarrassed about her T-shirt to even notice. He'd thought Serena would be nervous walking the runway with all those supermodels. He'd thought she'd need his moral support, but it was pretty obvious she was having the time of her life. She probably got a thrill out of hearing everyone in the tent whispering her name. Not him. Sure, he wanted to be famous—a famous *rock star*. Not famous for being the boy on Serena's I LOVE AARON T-shirt.

He reached in his coat pocket and pulled out his half-empty tin of herbal cigarettes. Before he could even open the tin, a security guard put his hand on his shoulder.

"No smoking in the tents, sir."

Fuck this, Aaron mumbled under his breath. But he couldn't just get up and leave while Serena was still onstage. He glanced at Blair in the seat next to him. She was biting her lip and clutching her stomach like she had gas or something.

Blair wanted to cover her diamond-studded ears to block out the sound of everyone whispering Serena's name. *Those eyes! Those legs! That fantastic hair!* It was completely nauseating, and the after-party was bound to be just more of the same. As soon as Serena skipped down the runway path marked TO GRANDMOTHER'S HOUSE and off the stage to change outfits, Blair stood up to go.

"I think I'm going to take off before the snow gets too fucking deep," she announced to Aaron.

"Yeah?" Aaron jumped to his feet. "I'll help you find a cab." Serena didn't need him around. She'd probably be so surrounded by admirers during the after-party, he wouldn't even get a chance to see her. She wouldn't mind if he just quietly took off.

Outside in Bryant Park the snow was already ankle deep. The lion statues on the steps of the public library looked even larger and more menacing blanketed in white.

"Think I'll just hop a train up to Scarsdale," Aaron said, referring to the Westchester suburb where he'd lived with his mom before deciding to move in with his dad's new family in the city last fall. He flicked open his Zippo and lit an herbal cigarette. "My buddies and I always get together out on the golf course when there's a big storm like this. It's a good time."

"Sounds like a fucking blast," Blair replied disinterestedly.

Fat, frozen flakes of snow landed on her mascara-coated lashes and she squinted her eyes, burying her hands in her black cashmere Les Best evening coat pockets as she searched for a cab. *Fuck,* it was freezing.

"Want to come with me?" Aaron offered, even though Blair had been a total bitch lately. They were still stepbrother and stepsister—they could at least try to be friends.

Blair grimaced. "No, thanks. I'm going to call this man I met. See if he wants to meet me somewhere for a drink or something." She loved how the word *man* sounded so much more sophisticated than *guy*.

"What *man*?" Aaron asked suspiciously. "Not that old dude from Yale you were with last night?"

Blair stamped her feet to keep her toes from getting frostbitten inside her totally-wrong-for-the-weather Les Best Mary Janes. Why did Aaron always have to act so infuriatingly superior? "First of all, I could be meeting someone else. Second of all, what do you care anyway? And third of all, if it is him, so *what*?" She flung her hand in the air and waved it impatiently. It was only nine. Where the hell were all the fucking cabs?

Aaron shrugged. "I don't know. I'm just guessing he's like some big investment banker who gives lots of cash to Yale, and you're flirting with him or whatever because you want to get in so badly. Which is pretty lame if you ask me."

"Actually, I didn't ask," Blair snapped back. "But maybe I *should* listen to Mr. Accepted-Early-At-Harvard-Even-Though-All-I-Do-Is-Sit-Around-In-My-Underwear-Drinking-Beer-And-Pretending-I-Play-In-A-Really-Cool-Band-Which-Actually-Sucks, since you obviously know everything." A taxi screeched to a stop at the corner of Forty-third Street to let someone out. Blair made a dash for it. "Don't fucking make judgments about something you know nothing about!" she shouted at Aaron, before jumping into the cab and pulling the door shut.

Aaron shivered in his thin cotton jacket and hunched his shoulders into the bitter wind as he walked east on Forty-second Street to Grand Central Station. It would be good to just hang with the guys for a change. Women were a monumental pain in his vegan ass.

But we're oh, so worth it—right?

way better than naked

Dan tried not to stare at the models as they came out onto the runway during the Better Than Naked show wearing only pleated brown corduroy miniskirts with no tops on at all. Their skirts were so short he could even see the frilly white panties they were wearing underneath, which happened to be little girls' vintage underwear from the nineteen-fifties and fit so snugly on the models that their butt cheeks were busting out of them. Instead of sitting down in the front row, where Rusty Klein had managed to snag him a seat between Stevie Nicks and superhip performance artist Vanessa Beecroft, Dan stood at the back of the Harrison Street Club, clutching his black leather bound notebook and trying to look writerly in case Rusty Klein was somewhere nearby and was secretly studying him.

The show was set to strange German folk music and there was straw scattered on the runway. Little boys with blond pageboy haircuts wearing lederhosen led bleating white goats around by leather leashes as impossibly tall models stomped by them, their bare breasts bobbing.

Bestiality, Dan scribbled furtively in his notebook. The goats were crapping all over the place and he noticed that the hems of the models' skirts had been shredded on purpose.

Tears were drawn on their cheeks in iridescent blue eye pencil. *Ruined milkmaids*, Dan wrote, trying not to feel completely out of place. What the hell was he doing at a fashion show anyway?

The twenty-something-year-old brunette next to him leaned over and tried to read what he was writing. "Who are you with?" she demanded. "*Nylon? Time Out?*" She was wearing pointy rhinestone-studded glasses fastened old-lady style to a gold chain around her neck and had the thickest bangs Dan had ever seen. "Why aren't you seated with press?"

Dan closed his black notebook before she could read any more. "I'm a poet," he said importantly. "Rusty Klein invited me."

The woman didn't seem that impressed. "What have you published lately?" she asked suspiciously.

Dan tucked his notebook under his arm and smoothed down his new set of sideburns. One of the goats had gotten loose and jumped off the runway. Four security guards ran after it. "Actually, one of my more recent poems is in this week's issue of *The New Yorker*. It's called 'Sluts.'"

"No way!" the woman gushed in a loud whisper. She pulled her lavender leather Better Than Naked tote bag into her lap and retrieved her copy of *The New Yorker*. Flipping through it, she turned to page forty-two. "You don't understand. I read this poem over the phone to *all* my girlfriends. I can't believe you wrote it."

Dan didn't know what to say. This was his first encounter with an actual fan and he felt simultaneously embarrassed and thrilled. "I'm glad you liked it," he replied modestly.

"Liked it?" the woman repeated. "It changed my life! Would you mind signing this for me?" she asked, thrusting the magazine into his lap.

Dan shrugged and retrieved his pen. *Daniel Humphrey*, he

scribbled just beside his poem, but his signature looked a little plain and impersonal so he added a squiggly little flourish underneath it. He'd scribbled over a few lines of the Gabriel Garcia Rhodes story, which seemed kind of like sacrilege, but who really cared, when he'd just signed his first autograph. He was famous—a real, genuine writer!

"Thank you *so, so* much," the woman said, taking the magazine back. She pointed to his notebook. "Now you go ahead and keep writing," she whispered reverently. "Forget I bothered you."

German folk music morphed into opera and the little boys left the runway leading their goats. Models floated in wearing long black wool capes, peacock blue suede thigh-high boots, and ostrich feather headdresses. They looked like characters out of a *Lord of the Rings* sequel.

Dan flipped open his notebook and began to write. *Good and bad witches,* he scribbled. *Hunting hungry wolves.* He bit the end of his pen and then added, *Wish I could smoke a fucking cigarette.*

v poses as a poser

For her appearance at the Culture of Humanity by Jedediah Angel show at Highway 1 in Chelsea, Vanessa broke her tradition of wearing only black and borrowed Ruby's red scoop-neck top with three-quarter-length sleeves. It was the same top she'd worn once before and gotten a lot of compliments on, probably because it was so low it revealed her soft, pale cleavage and a hint of her black lace bra. Vanessa had arrived late because her sister had insisted she take a cab, and of course the cab had gotten stuck in the snow near Union Square. While the driver yelled at the towing company on his cell phone with Lite FM blaring from the speakers, Vanessa had jumped ship. When she'd finally made it to the club, her ears had been frozen solid and she'd looked like a walking snowball. The fashion show had already started and she'd been sure they'd turn her away at the huge garage door that served as an entrance, but when she'd given her name to the girl at the door, a security guard with a flashlight had been appointed to personally escort Vanessa to her seat in the *center* of the *front row*. The chair had a card taped to it with CHRISTINA RICCI crossed out in black marker and VANESSA ABRAMS written in instead. Vanessa had never felt so special in all her life.

The room was dark except for burning white foot-high candles lining the runway on either side. Models dressed in navy blue above-the-knee sailor dresses with white piping and gold buttons at the lapels held foghorns to their lips as the sound of a terrible storm at sea boomed out of the sound system. The white wall behind the runway was lit with a single spotlight, and on that wall was projected the New York film essay Vanessa had sent to NYU. The film was black and white and it took on a sort of nineteen-forties classiness paired with the models' sailor dresses. And even though everyone there seemed to be taking this whole bogus fashion-at-sea thing way too seriously, Vanessa had to admit it was pretty cool to see her film up there in lights.

The wafer-thin woman next to her flipped open her PalmPilot and typed in, *Brilliant backdrop*, with a long red fingernail. She was wearing an ID tag on her camel-colored cashmere sweater with the word *Vogue* printed on it, and her brown hair was cut in a short bob with thick, bronze-highlighted bangs. She continued to type. *Note: Ask Jed where the film came from.*

Vanessa considered nudging her gently and saying, "I made it," but she decided it would be more fun to stay quiet and see what happened. Maybe someone would detest the film and make a big stink about it and Vanessa would become known as the infamous filmmaker whose bitterly honest portrayal of New York had been a real downer at Fashion Week. She wondered how Dan was doing at the Better Than Naked show. She imagined him asking that hot new Brazilian supermodel—Anike, or whatever her name was—for a light without even knowing who she was. That was the thing Vanessa most loved about Dan, his divine innocence.

The film came to the part where she'd filmed two old men wearing matching red-and-black plaid wool jackets and black wool caps playing chess in Washington Square Park. One guy's head bobbed against his chest, his burning cigar perched precariously on his sagging lower lip as he began to fall asleep. The other guy snapped his fingers to make sure his partner was asleep before moving the chess pieces around and nudging his sleeping friend awake again.

Inside Highway 1 the sounds of the storm faded and boisterous big-band music began to play. A giant cardboard boat was hauled onto the stage by muscular male models pulling thick white ropes and wearing only simple navy blue briefs. The boat came to a stop and the gangplank was lowered. Out came the models, two at a time—there must have been a hundred of them, and how had they all fit into that boat?—all dressed in navy blue satin bra-and-panty sets, with white fishnet over-the-knee stockings, white elbow-length gloves and white suede over-the-knee boots. After marching down the gangplank with military-style efficiency they began a complicated dance that looked like a cross between air traffic control and water ballet. Suddenly the neat rows of gesticulating models parted to reveal a dapper dude with curly, shoulder-length red hair, wearing a white three-piece suit, carrying a jewel-encrusted gold cane, and *tap-dancing*.

No joke.

Red curls bouncing, he tap-danced right up to the end of the runway, stopped on a dime, and began to applaud the audience. Behind him the models stood on one leg, with the other knee raised high, like flamingos, applauding, too. Then the music stopped and the audience went wild.

The redhead had to be Jedediah Angel, Vanessa decided, and he was standing directly in front of her. He took a deep bow, looking a bit like the Wizard of Oz in his tight white suit. Suddenly he pointed at her and began to whoop and clap, motioning for her to stand up. Vanessa shook her head, alarmed, but Jedediah Angel kept on beckoning to her. "Stand up, baby! Stand *up!*"

The crowd was going crazy now. They didn't even know who the hell Vanessa was, but if Jedediah Angel wanted her to bow, she must be *somebody*. Giving in, Vanessa stood up, her face burning with embarrassment and her shoulders shaking in an uncharacteristically nervous fit of the giggles as she bowed her head to acknowledge their applause.

She could already hear Ken Mogul whispering in her ear, "Get used to it baby, you've rocked their world!" And even though it *was* kind of cool to have so many people acting like they worshipped her, she couldn't wait to trade stories with Dan about what a farce the whole thing was.

Unless of course he'd already eloped to the south of France with a hot nineteen-year-old Brazilian supermodel.

topics ◀ *previous*　*next* ▶　*post a question*　**reply**

Disclaimer: All the real names of places, people, and events have been altered or abbreviated to protect the innocent. Namely, me.

hey people!

Let it snow!

There are fourteen inches on the ground so far and here I am, snowed in at the hottest, most exclusive Fashion Week after-party ever, with my all-time favorite fashion designer, hundreds of gorgeous models and hunk-o-licious actors, the most discerning fashion magazine editors in the business, and five of fashion's most avant-garde photographers. I honestly don't care if the whole city shuts down because of the snow. I never want to leave!

Sightings

B waiting for her date in the corner of that romantic little bar in the new boutique hotel on Perry Street. **S** signing autographs at the **Les Best** after-party at **Crème** on Forty-third. **C** at the same party, surrounded by younger male models, also signing autographs—who is he pretending to be? **N** escorting our favorite Connecticut heiress home to her Greenwich mansion in her limo. **J** and her new best friend dashing through the snow to collect booty from Blockbuster and Hunan Wok on Broadway near J's house—sounds like a party. **D** being swarmed by models at the **Better Than Naked** after-party at the **Harrison Street Club**. Were they just bumming cigarettes or did they all actually read his poem? **V** at the **Jedediah Angel** after-party at **Highway 1**, pretending to flirt with everyone in that delightfully banal way of hers.

I just hope everyone is as ecstatic as I am about being stuck where they are until the weather clears. Remember, nothing warms you up faster than another person's body heat.

Oops, someone's taking my photograph for the Style section this weekend, and my lips are in serious need of some shine. Gotta fly!

You know you love me.

just like that scene in titanic

"So how come Dan didn't invite you?" Elise asked as she rolled a steamed dumpling around in a puddle of soy sauce.

To weather the snowstorm, Elise and Jenny had gathered a feast of Chinese food and Oreos and videos they'd never heard of, since everything else at Blockbuster had been rented out. Now they were watching the New York Fashion Week coverage on the Metro Channel in the living room of Jenny's sprawling, ramshackle Upper West Side apartment. Bizarrely enough, the camera had just panned over the audience at the Better Than Naked show, zooming in on Dan for a moment as he scribbled away furiously in his stupid black notebook.

"Because I'm his little sister," Jenny answered, stunned that she'd actually just seen her brother's sallow, sideburned face live on TV. She'd known Dan was going to the show, but she hadn't even bothered to ask if she could accompany him. He was so obsessed with being Mr. I'm-The-Next-Keats that he barely even noticed her existence anymore.

The camera shifted to the Les Best tent in Bryant Park, where Serena van der Woodsen strutted down the runway wearing a cropped white baby tee with I LOVE AARON printed on it, her gray Constance Billard School uniform skirt, a red wool cape, and Les Best ankle boots. It looked like she was supposed to be a sexy version of Little Red Riding Hood or something.

Not that anyone would *ever* pay money for a school uniform.

"Hey, isn't that our peer group leader? Serena van der Woodsen?" Elise pointed out.

Jenny stuffed an entire Oreo into her mouth and nodded, her cheeks bulging. It was Serena all right. Looking as perfect as ever.

"Quick, change the channel! There's no way I can eat anything while I'm looking at those legs," Elise squealed, tossing a beaded velvet throw pillow at the television.

Jenny giggled and turned off the TV altogether. She picked up her I Love NY mug of Coke, glancing warily at the feast spread out on the old steamer trunk that served as a coffee table. The apartment was so filthy, she worried that at any moment a disgusting lobster-sized cockroach would drop out of the crumbling plaster in the ceiling, right into her cold sesame noodles. She noticed Elise hadn't actually ingested any food yet. "You don't have a problem eating in front of me, do you?" Jenny picked up a pair of chopsticks and twirled them around in the cardboard container of noodles. "I promise I won't even look at you."

Elise picked up her dumpling with her fingers and bit it in half. "That's just in the lunchroom at school," she said with her mouth full. "I can't eat with all those skinny girls looking at my fat."

"You're not fat," Jenny responded, even though being around Elise actually gave her an appetite because she felt so tiny in comparison. Still, it was kind of a relief to see that Elise didn't have a real eating disorder, she was just insecure.

That was the thing about making a new friend—you were never quite sure if you totally *knew* them or not.

"Did you paint that?" Elise asked, pointing to the oil portrait Jenny had painted of her father, which was hanging over the mantel. Rufus was wearing a white V-neck undershirt with cigarette burns in it, and he hadn't shaved in days. His wiry gray hair stuck out in all directions, and his hazel eyes were wild with caffeine-induced excitement and from doing too much acid in the sixties. It was a pretty accurate portrait.

"Yup." Jenny wound more noodles around her chopsticks. She hadn't painted anything since the portraits she'd done of Nate in December. She'd painted his face in every style she'd studied. There was Picasso Nate, Monet Nate, Dali Nate, Warhol Nate, and Pollock Nate. But when Nate had broken her heart, she'd burned them all in a metal trash can out on West Ninety-ninth Street. It had been a moment of catharsis—their love turned to ashes. Actually, now that she thought about it, she should have saved the ashes and made something with them—a self-portrait or a calming seascape—but it was too late now.

Elise reached for yet another dumpling. "Will you paint me?" she asked.

Jenny glanced out the smudged living room window. The snow was so thick, it looked like someone was exploding giant down pillows in the sky. "Sure," she said, standing up to get her paints. It wasn't like she had anything better to do.

"Cool!" Elise tossed the remains of the dumpling back into the container and unbuttoned her too-tight Seven jeans. Then she pulled her pink Gap turtleneck over her head, taking her pull-on crop-top bra with it. When Jenny returned with a clean white canvas and her palette of oils, Elise was sprawled out on the couch, her wiry blonde hair dusting her freckled shoulders, completely naked.

"What are you doing?" Jenny demanded, mystified.

Elise stretched her arms over her head and settled her head back against the throw pillows. "I've always wanted to pose nude," she said. "You know, like that scene in the movie *Titanic*."

Jenny sat down cross-legged on the floor opposite her and wetted her brush. "Whatever," she remarked, frowning at her eager, voluptuous subject.

Maybe her new friend was less insecure than she'd first thought. And a lot crazier, too.

some like it hot

Blair sat at a corner table in the downstairs bar of Red, the new cozily romantic Perry Street boutique hotel, drinking Absolut and tonic and trying not to watch the coverage of Fashion Week on the Metro Channel. It seemed like every time she looked up they were showing the same clip of Serena prancing around the runway at the Les Best show wearing her school uniform and that stupid I LOVE AARON T-shirt. Even in the bar, she could hear people murmuring, "Who is she?" and "Who's Aaron?" It was enough to drive Blair right up the red velvet–covered wall.

"I wore my Yale tie this time," Owen announced with a sly grin as he strode through the door wearing a tan Burberry trench coat and a black wool fedora hat that made him look even more manly and dashing than when she'd first met him. He slid into the red velvet–covered bench next to Blair and kissed her on the cheek. His face was damp and cold from the storm, and the feel of it against her face made her whole body tingle. "Hello, gorgeous."

Instantly Blair forgot all about Serena. She was with a sexy older man who called her "gorgeous." *So there.*

"Hi." She twisted her ruby ring around and around on her

ring finger. "I'm sorry I dragged you out on a night like this. I was just so . . . *bored*."

The cocktail waitress came over and Owen ordered a Bombay Sapphire martini straight up. He pulled a pack of Marlboro Lights from his pocket, put two cigarettes in his mouth, lit them both and passed one to Blair. His black eyebrows furrowed with brooding concern as he gazed at her with his piercingly bright blue eyes. "You're not in any trouble, are you?"

Trouble? Blair took a drag off her cigarette and considered her answer. If you could call having a crush on your older, married Yale alum interviewer trouble, then yes, she was in *terrible* trouble. "Maybe," she replied coyly. "Are you?"

The waitress brought Owen his martini. He ate the green olive floating inside it and then wiped his mouth with a cocktail napkin. A trace of dark five o'clock shadow cloaked his sharply defined chin. "I was in a breakfast meeting this morning, eating Cheerios with five other lawyers, and I was thinking about you," he admitted.

Blair ran her fingernail over her fishnet-stockinged knee. "Really?" she asked, immediately wishing her voice didn't sound quite so eager and hopeful.

Owen raised his glass to his lips, his blue eyes smoldering. "Yeah. I've been so crazy busy this week, but I promise I'll get that report over to the guys at Yale ASAP."

"Oh," Blair responded disappointedly. She twirled her little brown cocktail straw around in her drink. For once she hadn't even been thinking about Yale. Being with Owen made her feel like she was *beyond* Yale. She was his "gorgeous," the star of his show. Or maybe she was only deluding herself.

Glancing through the paned glass window behind them, Blair could barely see the cars parked out on the street. They were just masses of white, like big, dumb sleeping elephants.

She could feel Owen watching her as she puffed on her cigarette and blew a stream of gray smoke into the air above their heads. He'd asked to see her again, hadn't he? And he wouldn't have done that if he wasn't attracted to her. He was just nervous, that was all. Inside Blair's head, the cameras were starting to roll. She was the femme fatale seducing the handsome, good, older lawyer. Yale was the last thing she wanted to talk about right now.

She took one last puff on her cigarette and then stubbed it out in the chrome ashtray in the center of the table. "I almost went to jail once," she announced, trying to sound intriguing.

This wasn't exactly true. A few months ago she'd stolen a pair of cashmere pajamas from Barneys' men's department to give to Nate as a surprise gift when they were having problems. But when they'd broken up for real, Serena had convinced Blair to put the pajamas back. She'd never even gotten caught.

Owen chuckled and picked up his drink. He was wearing gold cuff links with a blue *Y* stamped on them to match his blue-and-gold Yale tie. "See, you're just the kind of girl Yale needs," he joked.

"And I'm a virgin," Blair blurted out, fluttering her eyelashes at the randomness of her remark. It was strange. Even though Owen was extremely dashing and she really wanted to see what it felt like to kiss him, she was a little afraid of what she was doing.

"I'm sure Yale needs more of those, too," Owen laughed. He crossed and then uncrossed his legs and Blair could see she was making him nervous, which wasn't what she'd intended.

She reached under the table and slipped her small, trembling fingers over his warm, tanned hand. "I don't mind if you kiss me," she murmured in a low, breathy voice that sounded exactly like Marilyn Monroe in *Some Like It Hot*.

Owen put down his drink. "Come here," he said gruffly, wrapping his free arm around her and pulling her toward him.

His chin was rough and scratched Blair's face as they kissed, but she'd never been kissed so expertly and powerfully in all her life. Plus he smelled faintly of Hermès Eau d'Orange Verte, which was her all-time favorite men's cologne.

Blair had thought she'd be plagued by guilt the moment their lips met. *He's a friend of Dad's,* she reminded herself. *He's* old. But Owen was such a good kisser, now that he'd started, she wasn't about to make him stop.

s can't find her boyfriend, but so what?

"I told her she has a better backside than any girl in the business," one of Les Best's stylists told a photographer for *W* magazine. "That slim-hipped, tomboy butt. Like she could just slip on her boyfriend's dirty old jeans and make them look fresh and sexy."

Serena shook her lovely blond head in good-natured protest and puffed on an American Spirit. "My boyfriend never wears jeans. He thinks they're overrated. He wears those green canvas army pants. You know, the real ones from the army surplus store?" She glanced around the crowded, smoky after-party which was in full force at Crème, a new go-go club on Forty-third Street, but she didn't see Aaron anywhere. He'd never come backstage at the show, so she'd figured she'd just meet him here.

"And is your boyfriend named Aaron, by any chance?" the stylist asked. He giggled and pointed at her T-shirt. "You should get Les to make a whole line of those. Everyone would totally go for it—it would be so wild!"

"Would you mind stepping back for a moment so I could get her picture?" the photographer asked the stylist.

"And could you autograph this Polaroid for my collection,

Serena?" a tiny leather-pants-wearing older man with a white buzz cut asked.

"Me too!" another voice chimed in.

Serena hitched up the baby blue hip-hugging Les Best jeans she'd acquired compliments of the house and pointed to the I LOVE AARON logo emblazoned on the front of her shirt as she grinned cheesily for the camera.

"I bet if you held an auction for that shirt right now, you could sell it for a thousand dollars," the photographer quipped as he snapped away. "But of course you'd never part with it."

Serena took another puff on her cigarette as the group around her waited for her to respond. The T-shirt was cute, but it was really just a spur-of-the-moment thing she'd done because she'd thought Aaron would think it was funny and to make it up to him for appearing in a fashion show on a Friday night, *their* night. She was a spur-of-the-moment kind of gal, which was exactly why this auction idea sounded so appealing. She could give the money to a good cause like Little Hearts, that children's charity the Valentine's Day ball money was supposed to go to.

"Let's do it," she giggled giddily.

The group of admirers whooped with delight and followed her over to the bar like adoring little mice following the Pied Piper.

"Who wants to buy a T-shirt?" Serena crowed, jumping up on top of the bar, and parading up and down like she was on the runway again.

Of course only someone as gorgeous as she was could actually get away with this.

The DJ joined in the fun, putting on Madonna's old classic, "Vogue," and turning the volume all the way up. Serena shook her booty and stuck out her chest—it was all in good fun—as every pair of eyes in the club tuned in to watch.

"Five hundred dollars!" someone shouted.

"Anyone else?" Serena taunted the dazzled crowd. "It's for a good cause."

"Seven hundred!"

"Eight!"

Serena stopped dancing, rolled her eyes and whipped her cigarettes out of her pocket, as if to say, "Your stinginess bores me." The crowd laughed and fifteen or so lighters were offered her way. She bent down to grab a light from a lucky dude wearing a fur vest, and then pranced away again, shaking her hips to the music and puffing away as she waited for the bidding to go up.

"A thousand dollars!" the dude wearing the fur vest shouted. He'd gotten close enough to Serena to know that it was worth it.

Serena threw her arms in the air and whooped loudly, daring someone to take the bidding to new heights. As much as she hated to admit it, she didn't even mind that Aaron hadn't turned up. She might have loved him, but she was having a kick-ass time without him.

romancing the stoner

"We can ask the butler to take his clothes off and play the piano for us," Georgie told Nate. "He does whatever I tell him to."

When group therapy had been over and it was time for the outpatients to go home, the storm had already been so bad, Nate couldn't get a car to take him to the station, so Georgie had offered to give him a ride. Then when they'd gotten to the station the trains had stopped running, so the ever-accommodating Georgie had taken Nate home to her house in her bodyguard-driven black Range Rover. Now they were sitting on the floor of her enormous, luxurious bedroom, getting stoned as they watched the snow pile up on the skylight overhead.

The Upper East Side town house Nate had grown up in was four stories high and had its own elevator and a twenty-four-hour cook. But Georgie's Greenwich, Connecticut, mansion had something his family's town house didn't—vast amounts of space inside, and acres of land around the house. It was like a city unto itself, and Georgie had her own private borough where she could do absolutely whatever she pleased while her ancient English nanny was in bed watching BBC America and the other servants were doing their jobs in the other boroughs. Georgie's bathroom even had a Roman daybed in it for lounging on while she waited for her twelve-foot-wide marble Jacuzzi to fill up.

"Or we could have crazy loud sex on the stairs," Georgie added. "That would really drive the staff nuts."

Nate leaned his head back against the footboard of Georgie's four-poster king-sized bed and put the joint they were sharing to his lips. "Let's just watch the snow fall for a while."

Georgie rolled over on her back, resting her head on the leg of Nate's navy blue Culture of Humanity ripstop trousers. "God, you're mellow. I'm not used to hanging out with some-one so mellow."

"What are your friends like?" Nate asked, sucking hard on the joint. Pot seemed to taste and feel better now that he'd gone without it for a while.

"I don't have any friends anymore," Georgie answered. "They all kind of gave up on me because I'm so nuts."

Nate put his hand on her head and began stroking her hair. She had incredibly soft, luxurious hair. "I hang out a lot with these three guys in my class at school," he said, referring to Jeremy, Anthony, and Charlie. "But I went for a few days without getting high and I didn't really want to hang out with them, you know?"

"That's what Jackie calls a 'negative friendship.' A 'positive friendship' is when you do fun, constructive things with your friends like baking cookies, making collages, and climbing mountains."

"I'm your friend," Nate offered quietly.

Georgie rubbed the back of her head against his leg. "I know." She laughed, her not-too-small chest jiggling up and down inside her tight white T-shirt. "Want to bake some cookies?"

Nate combed a lock of her hair up into the air with his fingers and then let it fall, strand by strand, back into his lap. Blair had long hair, too, but it wasn't as straight or as silky as Georgie's. It was funny how girls could all be so different. "Can I kiss you?" he asked, not really having intended to sound so formal.

"Okay," Georgie whispered.

Nate bent over and brushed his lips against the bridge of her nose, her chin, and finally her lips. She kissed him back hungrily and then pulled away and sat up on her elbows. "This is what Jackie calls 'feeding your craving.' You're doing something that feels good temporarily instead of 'healing the wounds.'"

Nate shrugged. "Why is it temporary?" He pointed up at the skylight, which was completely smothered in snow. "I'm not going anywhere."

Georgie scooched her feet up under her and stood up. She disappeared into the bathroom and Nate could hear a cabinet door open and the sounds of pill bottles rattling and water running. Then she came out, brushing her teeth, her light brown eyes all lit up like she'd just had an epiphany, or at the very least a good idea. "There's an old carriage up in the attic. We can go up and sit in it," she announced with her mouth full of toothpaste. She went back into the bathroom to spit and then came out again, holding a pale hand out to Nate. "Are you coming?"

Nate stood up and took her hand. His body was humming from the pot and the intense smoothness of Georgie's skin. All he really wanted to do was to kiss her some more. "Can I 'feed my craving' when we get up there?" he asked, feeling very stoned indeed.

Georgie cocked a thin dark eyebrow at him and licked her dark red lips. "I might even let you 'heal my wounds.'"

Nate grinned his lopsided stoner grin. Who'd known rehab psychobabble could be such a turn-on!

our bodies, ourselves

"My hand is getting tired," Jenny complained to Elise after she'd painted Elise's head and neck. "I'll do the rest tomorrow."

"Let's see," Elise said, sitting up. Her chest was so small Jenny couldn't help but stare at it. Her breasts were like the little new potatoes her dad had grown when they'd rented a house in Pennsylvania one summer. Small, hard, and beigey pink. "It looks good," Elise said, squinting at the canvas. "But how come you made my face green?"

Jenny hated when people asked her questions about her art. She didn't know why she did what she did, she just did it. And her dad always said, "The artist doesn't have to answer to anyone but himself." Or *her*self, in her case. "Because I was in a green mood," she answered, annoyed.

"Well, green is my favorite color," Elise responded happily. She pulled on her turtleneck and underwear but left her jeans and bra on the floor. "Oh my God. I have that book, too!" she squealed, pointing at a thick, heavy paperback on the bookshelf behind the TV. She walked over to the shelf and pulled the book out. "But yours is so new. Don't you ever read it?"

Jenny bit off the top of an Oreo and read the title on the spine of book. *The New This Is My Body for Women.* "My dad bought me that last year. I think he probably thought that if I read it, he wouldn't have to explain anything to me about sex—I could just look up the embarrassing stuff."

"But have you ever actually looked at it? Some of it is really *graphic*."

Jenny had no idea. She'd immediately shelved the book behind the TV along with the other random books her father had given her that she never intended to read, like *Breathing Room: A Buddhist's Guide to Living Creatively, Mao's Secret Seven: The Women Behind Chairman Mao,* and *Finding the Dragon Within: What Is Your Art?*

"Like, graphic in what way?" Jenny asked, intrigued.

Elise carried the book over to the worn leather sofa and sat down, crossing her long bare legs dramatically. "I'll show you." She opened the book and Jenny sat down next to her and leaned in close to see.

The first thing Elise turned to was a detailed diagram of a woman on her hands and knees bent over a man lying on his back. The book had been written in the nineteen-seventies and the text had since been updated, but the diagrams hadn't. The man had hair down to his shoulders, a full beard, and was wearing beads. His penis was sticking straight up and it appeared to be in the woman's mouth. The two girls erupted into giggles.

Ew!

"I told you," said Elise, pleased with herself for opening right up to such a gem.

"I can't believe I never saw any of this," Jenny exclaimed. She grabbed the book away from Elise and rifled through the pages. "Oh my God!" she gasped when she saw a diagram of the same couple in another position. The woman still had the long-haired guy's penis in her mouth, except this time she was lying alongside him with her feet up around his head and her legs splayed so that he could do the same thing to *her*. Jenny didn't even know the name for *that*. "I thought this was just a boring book about getting your period and all that stuff. But this is, like, a real *sex* book for *women*."

"I think there's a teen one, too, that's totally boring, but my mom got me this one by mistake. I couldn't believe it when I started reading it!"

The two girls pored over the pages until they stumbled upon a section called Same-Sex Relationships.

"Like Ms. Crumb," Jenny observed, reading. The introduction was long and started with the line, "Your feelings are genuine and not to be ignored. . . ." Outside she could hear the grating sound of a snowplow driving by. She looked up to watch the snow falling steadily through the grimy living room window.

"Hey. You want to try it?" Elise asked.

Jenny turned back to the book. "What?"

"Kissing," Elise answered in barely a whisper.

Your feelings are genuine and not to be ignored.

Yes, but Jenny didn't really have any feelings for Elise. She liked her and everything but she wasn't *attracted* to her. Still, kissing a girl sounded exciting. It was something she'd never done before, and if it felt uncomfortable, she could always pretend to be kissing that tall blond boy she'd spotted in Bendel's.

She closed the book and folded her hands in her lap. Her face was only inches away from Elise's. "Okay, let's do it." It was just an experiment, something new to try on a boring, snowy night.

Elise leaned forward and put her hand on Jenny's arm. Then she closed her eyes and Jenny closed hers, too. Elise pressed her lips against Jenny's tightly clenched mouth. It wasn't a kiss exactly—it was too *dry*. It felt more like a nudge or something.

Elise pulled her head back and both girls opened their eyes. "It says in the book to relax and enjoy yourself, especially when it's your first time."

What, had she, like, memorized the book?

Jenny pulled her curly brown hair up on top of her head and blew a big breath out through her nose. She didn't know what she was so nervous about, but she would have preferred it if Elise had still been wearing her pants. "Do you mind putting your jeans back on?" she asked. "I think I could, you know, relax more if you were like, dressed."

Elise hopped up and scooted into her jeans. "There, is that better?" she asked, leaving them unbuttoned as she sat down on the sofa again.

"Okay. Let's try it again," Jenny replied, revving herself up. She closed her eyes and slid her hands under Elise's hair and around her neck, trying to be less of a prude about the whole thing.

After all, she was an artist, and artists did all sorts of crazy things.

the next keats meets his next muse

After the Better Than Naked fashion show, the candles lining the runway were removed and red and blue strobe lights began to zoom against the black velvet walls. DJ Sassy broke out the phat French house beats, and the Harrison Street Club was transformed into a seventies European disco full of half-naked ninety-pound models drinking Cristal champagne straight out of the bottle.

Dan stood alone by the bar, sipping his Red Bull–and–who-knew-what-else cocktail. It tasted exactly like baby aspirin and he was only drinking it because the bartender had promised him it was loaded with caffeine and something called taurine, which was guaranteed to keep him hyperawake all night.

All of a sudden he noticed a violently tall woman wearing a flaming red bouffant wig—it *had* to be a wig—neon pink lipstick, and *huge* tortoise-shell sunglasses standing in the middle of the packed room with her hands cupped around her mouth. "Daniel Humphrey? Calling Daniel Humphrey!" she shrieked.

It was Rusty Klein.

Dan tilted his head back and downed his drink, blinking

his eyes as the caffeine and whatever else was in his drink rushed to his brain all at once. He stumbled over to the woman, his heart thumping even faster than the music. "I'm Dan," he croaked.

"*Look* at *you*! Our new *poet*! You're *adorable*! *Perfect*!" Rusty Klein pushed her enormous sunglasses up on top of her head and jangled the enormous gold bracelets covering her long bony wrists as she grabbed Dan and kissed each of his cheeks. Her perfume smelled oily and acidic, like tuna fish. "I love you, honey," she purred, squeezing Dan tight.

Dan shrank away, unused to being manhandled by someone he'd only just met. He hadn't expected Rusty Klein to be so *scary*. Her eyebrows had been dyed to match her wig and she was dressed like a sword fighter, in a form-fitting black velvet Better Than Naked puffy-sleeved jacket and matching black velvet bullfighting pants. A rope of black pearls clung to her pale, bony cleavage.

"I've been trying to write more poems," Dan stammered. "You know, for my book?"

"Wonderful!" Rusty Klein shouted, thrusting her lips at him again and probably smearing bright pink lipstick all over his face. "Let's make a lunch date sometime next week."

"Um, I've got school all day every day next week, but I get out at three-thirty."

"*School!*" Rusty screamed. "You're so *cute*! We can do tea then. Call my office and have Buckley, my assistant, set it up. Oh, fuck me!" She clasped Dan's arm with a clawlike hand. Her fingernails were at least three inches long and painted orangey pink. "There's someone here you absolutely *must* meet."

Rusty let go of Dan and held out her arms to receive a frail-looking girl with a long, sad face and dirty blond hair. The girl was wearing only a see-through light pink slip over her gaunt frame and her lank, waist-length hair was uncombed, as if she'd just gotten out of bed. "Mystery Craze, this is Daniel Humphrey. Daniel, this is Mystery," Rusty purred loudly. "Mystery, honey, you remember that poem I gave you to read? The one you said . . . Oh, fuck me. I'll let *you* tell him what you said. Now if you'll excuse me, I'm going to go lick my favorite designer's ass so he'll give me some new free clothes. Love you both. Ciao!" she added, before striding away in her five-inch black stilettos.

Mystery blinked her huge, tired gray eyes. She looked like she'd been up all night cleaning floors, like Cinderella. "Your poem saved my life," she confided to Dan in a low, husky voice. A tall, narrow glass of something bright red was wedged into her frail hand. "It's Campari," she said when she noticed him looking at it. "Want a taste?"

Dan never drank anything that wasn't caffeinated. He shook his head no and tucked his black notebook under his arm. Then he lit a Camel and took a long drag. There, that was much better. Now at least he'd have something to do, even if he couldn't think of anything to say. "So, are you a poet, too?" he asked.

Mystery stuck her thumb into her drink and then licked it off. The corners of her mouth were stained red with Campari, making her look like a little girl who'd just eaten a cherry Popsicle. "I write poems and short stories. And I'm working on a novel about cremation and premature death. Rusty says I'm the next Sylvia Plath," she answered. "What about you?"

Dan sipped his drink. He wasn't sure what she meant by premature death. Was there ever a right time to die? He wondered if he should write a poem about it, but then again, he didn't want to steal Mystery's material. "I'm supposed to be the next Keats."

Mystery dunked her thumb into her drink again and then licked it off. "What's your favorite verb?"

Dan took another drag off his cigarette and blew smoke into the crowded, noisy room. He wasn't sure if it was the club, or the music, or the caffeine, or the taurine, but he felt so alive and *so good* at that very moment, talking about words with this girl named Mystery whose life he had saved. He was seriously digging it.

"*Dying*, I guess," he answered, finishing his drink and setting the empty glass down on the floor. "The verb *to die*." He knew it must have sounded like he was trying to impress her. After all, she was writing a book about premature death and cremation. But it was the truth. Almost all of his poems really were about dying. Dying of love, dying of anger, dying of boredom, of anxiety; falling asleep and never waking up.

Mystery smiled. "Me too." Her gray eyes and long, thin face were starkly beautiful, but her front teeth were crooked and yellow, like she'd never been to the dentist in her entire life. She snagged another Red Bull cocktail from a waiter's tray and handed it to Dan. "Rusty says poets are the next movie stars. One day we'll both be riding around in limos with our bodyguards." She sighed heavily. "As if that will make life any easier." She raised her glass and clinked it against his. "To poetry," she announced grimly. Then she grabbed the back of Dan's head and pulled him toward her, crushing his lips in a deep, Campari-soaked kiss.

Dan knew he should have thrown Mystery off, protesting that he had a girlfriend, that he was in love. He shouldn't have enjoyed being hit on by a strange, practically naked girl with yellow teeth. But Mystery's lips tasted sweet and sour at the same time and he wanted to understand why she was so sad and so tired. He wanted to *discover* her, the way he sometimes discovered the perfect metaphor when he was in the middle of writing a poem, and to do that he had to keep kissing her.

"What's your favorite noun?" he breathed into her ear when he came up for air.

"*Sex*," she answered, diving for his lips again.

Dan grinned as he kissed her back.

It might have been the taurine, but sometimes it just feels good to be bad.

the girl behind the camera

"So you're the one." A beautiful, tanned, blond dude dressed in baggy orange surf shorts, white leather Birkenstock clogs, and a brown-and-white pony fur vest with nothing on underneath smiled at Vanessa with glistening white teeth. His name was Dork or Duke or something and he claimed to be a producer. "The genius filmmaker."

"She's the next Bertolucci," Ken Mogul corrected Duke, or whatever his name was. "Give me a year and she's going to be a household name." Ken was dressed like an urban cowboy in a silver Culture of Humanity down vest over a black Western-style shirt with pearly white snaps instead of buttons. His curly red hair was tucked into a black Stetson hat, and he was even wearing black cowboy boots with his Culture of Humanity boot-cut jeans. He'd flown into New York that night from Utah, where his most recent film had just been introduced at the Sundance Film Festival. It was an ambitious piece about a deaf and mute man who worked in a cannery in Alaska and lived in a trailer with thirty-six cats. The man didn't talk and spent a lot of time at his computer e-mailing girls on singles Web sites, so Ken had had to be extremely creative with the camera to keep the action going. It was his finest work yet.

"Dude, watching your film was like being born again," Dork told Vanessa. "It made my day."

The corners of Vanessa's mouth turned up in a half-bored, half-amused Mona Lisa smile. She wasn't sure how she felt about being called "dude," but she was glad she'd made Dork's day.

The Culture of Humanity by Jedediah Angel after-party was an even bigger deal than the fashion show itself. Highway 1 had been decorated like a Hindu wedding tent, and bikini-clad models who hadn't even been in the show were lounging on leather sofas, drinking saffron martinis, or dancing to the live bhangra music. Vanessa tugged on her tight red top. It was kind of hard not to feel like a porker around so many bony, seven-foot-tall models.

"Okay. Here's the guy from *Entertainment Weekly*," Ken Mogul said, wrapping his arm around her waist. "Smile, it's a photo op!"

Duke stood on the other side of Vanessa and pressed his tanned, angular cheek against her soft, pale one. He smelled like Coppertone. "Say salami!"

It was Vanessa's policy *not* to smile when she was being forced to have her picture taken, but why not? There really wasn't any danger that she'd get swept up in the glow, marry Duke in the Temple of Surf and Sand, and live cheesily ever after in a surf shack–cum–film studio on the beach in Malibu. She was too hard-core New York for that, and besides, she hated the beach. No, tonight would be her one night of cheese and then tomorrow she'd go back to being normal again.

"Salami!" all three of them cried, flashing their cheesiest smiles for the camera.

Duke stayed close to Vanessa's side after the photographer left. "What hotel are you staying at?" he asked, assuming she was from LA, just like everyone else he knew.

Vanessa unscrewed the cap on her bottle of Evian and took a swig. "Actually, I live here in New York, in Williamsburg, with my sister. I'm still in high school. She plays in a band."

Dork looked excited. "Dude!" he cried. "You're like one of those people screenwriters make up, you know?" He lifted his fingers to make quotations in the air, "An 'urban hipster.' Except you're *real*. You're realer than real. You're dyno-mite!"

For a guy called Dork, he was actually pretty insightful.

"Thanks," Vanessa said, unsure whether that was the correct response or not. She'd never had a conversation with someone so stupid before. She felt a hand on her elbow and she turned around.

A frail older man wearing a purple velvet smoking jacket and round black glasses smiled up at her. "You're the filmmaker, right?" he asked.

Vanessa nodded. "I guess."

The old man waggled a bony finger at her. "Don't take your gift too seriously," he said before wandering away.

Duke bent down and spoke urgently into her ear. "I'm staying at the Hudson. Wanna go back to my room for a drink or something?"

Vanessa knew she should have told him to fuck off, but she'd never been hit on by a gorgeous, dumb surfer dude who could have hit on any one of the models in the room but had chosen to hit on her instead. It was really kind of flattering. And hadn't that old guy just told her not to take things too seriously? Thank God she'd gone to all the trouble to remove the hair on her legs. "Maybe later," she replied, not wanting to shut Dork down completely. "It's kind of snowy out right now."

"Right, duh." Duke slapped himself on the head with a goofy laugh. "Want to dance instead?" He held out his hand, his arm muscles rippling invitingly. He looked like he never missed a workout and survived on a diet of protein drinks and wheatgrass.

Vanessa tugged on her red shirt again and took Duke's hand, following him out onto the throbbing, crowded dance floor. She couldn't believe herself—she *hated* to dance! At least no one she knew would be watching.

Oh yeah?

audrey keeps her clothes on

Because the snow had become completely unnavigable and they were trapped downtown, Blair decided that the most attractive option was to get a suite in the hotel upstairs.

"We can watch TV and order room service," she whispered enticingly in Owen's ear. "It'll be fun."

The room was luxurious, with a king-sized bed, a sunken Jacuzzi tub, a flat-screen plasma TV hanging on the wall, and an impressive view of the partially frozen, white-washed Hudson River. Owen called room service and ordered a bottle of Veuve Clicquot, filet mignon, pommes frites, and chocolate mousse cake, and when it came they lay on the bed, feeding each other cake and watching *Top Gun* on TNT.

"How come you and your wife split up?" Blair asked, forking a piece of cake into Owen's open mouth. Chocolatey crumbs fell onto the white 450-thread-count Egyptian cotton pillowcases.

Owen dipped a teaspoon into the cake's frosting and offered the spoon to Blair to lick off. "We haven't. . . ." He hesitated, his gorgeous, shapely eyebrows furrowing as he considered his answer. "I'd really rather not talk about it."

Blair smiled sympathetically as she let the frosting melt on her tongue. She liked playing the role of the other woman. It made her feel so . . . *powerful.* Across the room on the huge flat-screen TV Tom Cruise and Kelly McGillis were making out on his motorcycle. "Did she go to Yale, too?"

Owen picked up the remote and pointed it at the television. Then he put it down again without changing the channel. "I don't know," he replied, sounding exactly like Blair's little brother, Tyler, when he was watching TV and their mom asked if he'd done his homework yet.

Blair grabbed the remote and began flipping through the channels. A *Friends* rerun. Wrestling. MTV *Cribs.* She wasn't sure if she liked the boyish side of Owen. She much preferred the *man.* "She didn't go to Yale or she did?"

"Uh-huh," Owen answered, spooning a huge bit of cake into his mouth. "Astronomy major."

Blair raised her eyebrows as she watched Sean "P. Diddy" Combs give a tour of his Upper East Side manse. Owen's wife sounded like a genius. What kind of person became an astronomy major anyway? Someone who wanted to be an astronaut? She wished Owen had said his wife hadn't gone to college at all, but that she just sat around watching dog shows on TV and eating Krispy Kreme donuts. That in the end she'd weighed five hundred pounds and he'd been forced to sleep in the guest bedroom until eventually moving out altogether. There just hadn't been room for him anymore.

Blair flipped over to AMC, her favorite classic movie channel. *Casablanca,* starring Ingrid Bergman and Humphrey Bogart, was almost halfway through. The Germans had just invaded Paris and Ingrid was frightened.

She settled back on the pillows, missing the way her long hair used to fan out around her face in a way she imagined must have been irresistible. "Sometimes I pretend I'm living in those times," she told Owen dreamily. "It just seems so much more sophisticated, you know? No one wears jeans, everyone is so polite, and all the women have the best hairstyles."

"Yeah, but there was a war. A big one," Owen reminded her. He wiped his mouth on a white linen napkin and settled back against the pillows beside her.

"So?" Blair insisted. "It was still better."

Owen reached for her hand and Blair shifted her gaze away from the TV to study his profile. "You know you look exactly like Cary Grant?" she whispered.

"You think?" Owen turned his head to look at her, his blue eyes smoldering sexily.

"I cut my hair to look like Audrey Hepburn," Blair admitted. She turned on her side and rested her head against his manly chest in its crisp white shirt. "We could be Audrey and Cary."

Owen kissed her hair and squeezed her hand gently. "Here's looking at you, kid," he murmured. With his free hand he began to rub her back and Blair could feel his gold wedding band knock against the bumps in her spine.

Outside the snow was falling harder than ever. Blair watched it fall, unable to relax. It was sort of impossible not to think about Owen's genius astronaut wife, sitting home alone as she wrote out impossible astronomical equations on a blackboard, all the while wondering about her husband. Even if Blair and Owen did look exactly like Audrey Hepburn and Cary Grant, Blair was pretty sure the nice girls Audrey played didn't lose their virginities in hotel rooms with married older men, no matter how deep the snow got. Why not end the film here, while it was still good?

Owen was breathing deeply now and had stopped rubbing her back. As soon as Blair was sure he was asleep, she'd slip out the door and ask the concierge downstairs to call her a car home. After all, she had a reputation to maintain. And it wasn't like she was ditching him.

The best way to keep a guy intrigued is to disappear.

some girls have all the fun

"Snowball fight!" Serena cried at the top of her lungs to no one in particular. She'd been dancing with a pack of tipsy, half-naked Les Best models and her blond mane was matted to the back of her neck, creating a sort of unidreadlock, beach hair effect. She'd been relieved of her I LOVE AARON T-shirt for a cool four thousand bucks by her old friend Guy Reed from the Les Best boutique and was now wearing only a hot pink La Perla demibra that looked like a bikini top.

"Snow volleyball!" a guy shouted back even louder. He was dressed in a black ski suit from the Les Best ski line, black fur boots, and a pair of black fur earmuffs clung to his ears. He pointed out the huge bar windows to where a volleyball net had been set up outside on the snowy sidewalk.

In a matter of seconds the entire roomful of writhing, sweaty bodies attacked the coat closet, pulling on the nearest Fendi sheepskin or goose-down Gucci parka to protect their skinny bodies from the cold before they dashed outside to frolic in the snow.

Serena giggled as she slipped into a beige fleece-lined down parka with a beaver fur–trimmed hood that would have fit a giant Eskimo. In the last two hours she'd drunk more champagne than she had on New Year's Eve and she felt giddy and warm all over. Before she could even zip up her coat, someone grabbed her hand and pulled her out the door with him.

Outside the snow had enveloped everything and the streetlights glowed gold on the downy white blanket. Without the constant honk and roar of traffic, there was a pleasant calm about the city, as if it had finally gone to sleep. Shrieking in merriment, the gang of models, stylists, and photographers plowed through the thigh-deep drifts and began spiking balls over the volleyball net with total disregard for the peaceful scene.

"Isn't it beautiful?" Serena breathed. She wished Aaron were there so she could kiss him and tell him how much she loved him while stuffing a great big snowball down the back of his shirt. But he wasn't—the party pooper—so she would just have to make do. She turned to the guy holding her hand. It was the guy in the black ski suit, and he was tall, blond, and gorgeous. Everyone there was. She let go of his hand and scooped up a handful of snow. "Come here," she beckoned him. "I want to tell you a secret."

He took a step toward her, his breath filling the air with steamy clouds. "What?"

Serena stood on tiptoe and wrapped her arms around his neck. Then she kissed his cold, smooth cheek. "I love Aaron!" she squealed, stuffing the snowball down the back of his black ski suit and tearing off through the snow to join the others.

The guy chased after her, grabbing her legs and knocking her down just as they reached the volleyball net. The game was halted as the crowd of gorgeous revelers began to hurl snowballs at the frolicking pair, stopping now and then to light cigarettes or reapply their lip gloss before joining in again. Serena howled with laughter as snow went down the back of her jeans. That was the great thing about being so beautiful and so carefree. It didn't matter who you were with or what silly thing you were doing—you always had a fabulous time. In fact, you didn't even have to be in love with just one person when the world was already so in love with you.

experimentation may be overrated

Jenny and Elise were still kissing when Rufus called.

Ring, ring!

"Shit!" Jenny threw Elise off of her, leaped off the couch, and sprinted into the kitchen. It wasn't like anyone could see them, but she still felt like she'd been caught doing something incredibly embarrassing.

"Everything okay?" Rufus growled cheerfully into the phone. "I'm stuck down here with Max and Lyle and the rest of these losers. The snow's a bitch." Rufus spent most Friday nights down in the East Village at an old bar with his Communist writer friends. He sounded jolly, the way he always sounded when he'd had two or three glasses of red wine. "You girls staying out of trouble?"

Jenny blushed. "Uh-huh."

"Well, tell that friend of yours to stay put. No one in their right mind should try to get anywhere tonight."

Jenny nodded. "Okay." She'd been kind of hoping Elise would go home so she could take a hot bath and collect her thoughts, but she couldn't very well ask her to leave when there were four feet of snow on the ground and it was still coming down. "I'll see you later, Daddy," she said, almost wishing she could tell him how confused she was about what had just happened. She might have been a budding artist but that didn't mean she had to experiment *all* the time.

Jenny hung up the phone. "So what should we do now?" Elise asked, wandering into the kitchen with her jeans still unbuttoned. She separated an Oreo and licked the cream out of the inside.

Elise seemed to be hinting that she was ready to move on to the next chapter in *This Is My Body for Women*, but no *way* was Jenny going to find out what that entailed. She faked a yawn. "Dad says he's coming home soon," she lied. "I'm kind of tired anyway." She glanced out the kitchen window. Everything was white and the snow was still falling. It looked like the end of the world.

"Come on." She led the way to her bedroom. "Dad wants you to stay over." All she had was a single bed that she was definitely not sharing with Elise. Not when Elise was so . . . *horny* and unpredictable. "You can sleep on my bed and I'll sleep on the sofa."

"Okay," Elise replied dubiously. "I better call my mom. You're not mad at me are you?"

"Mad?" Jenny repeated casually. "Why would I be mad?" She pulled open her dresser drawer and handed Elise an oversized T-shirt and a pair of sweatpants. "Sleep in these," she directed. Otherwise Elise might decide to sleep in the nude, which would be very uncool, especially if Rufus came home later that night and barged into Jenny's room to give a senseless sermon on the meaning of life, as he was sometimes known to do when he'd drunk too much wine. She pulled out some pajamas for herself and closed the drawer. "I'm going to take a shower. You can use my cell phone if you want to call your mom."

Elise took the clothes and gazed up at the paintings on Jenny's wall. Over the bed was one of the Humphreys' cat, Marx, dozing on the stove, painted in thick oils. Marx was a deep turquoise color, and the stove was red. Near the window was a self-portrait of Jenny's feet, with her toenails painted orange and the bones in her feet painted blue.

"You're really good." Elise slipped her jeans down over her knees. "Don't you want to finish my portrait?"

Jenny grabbed her pink terrycloth bathrobe from the hook on the back of her door. "Not tonight," she responded, quickly heading down the hall to the bathroom. She'd take a long, hot shower, and hopefully by the time she came out Elise would be asleep. Tomorrow they would eat their Eggos and go sledding in the park and goof around like normal girls. No more experimentation. As far as Jenny was concerned, experimentation was completely overrated.

n facilitates recovery of messed-up orphan heiress

"Hold the reins in one hand and the whip in the other," Georgie instructed Nate. They were up in Georgie's attic, but instead of hanging out inside the gorgeous antique carriage and smoking dope and kissing and being mellow, Georgie was acting all hyperactive and making Nate *drive* the carriage.

The attic itself was incredible. It was full of beautiful old things from days gone by, but kept in perfect order as if at any time someone was going to carry them downstairs and put them to use again. The carriage was painted gold and lined with purple velvet, and under the seat inside, in a little leather chest, were fur rugs and muffs to keep your hands warm while you went out for a ride. Best of all, eight white carousel horses with white feather plumes affixed to real leather harnesses were pulling the carriage.

"Come on, faster, *faster*, giddyap, *giddyap*!" Georgie shouted at the carousel horses, cracking her long leather whip and bouncing up and down in the red leather coachman's seat.

Whoa.

Nate sat back on the seat beside her and tried to light another joint, but Georgie was bouncing around so much, it fell right out of his hand. "Fuck!" he cried, exasperated. He leaned over the side of the carriage to see where the joint had fallen on the white-painted wood floor, but the attic was lit only by a single dim bulb and he couldn't see the joint anywhere.

"That's okay." Georgie jumped down from the carriage. "Come on, there's something I want to show you."

Reluctantly Nate left the joint where it had fallen and followed her to the other side of the attic, where a bunch of antique wooden trunks were stacked. "This is where all my old horse stuff is kept," Georgie explained. She opened the top trunk and pulled out a handful of ribbons she'd won at horse shows. "I was a really good rider." She offered the ribbons to Nate.

All of them were blue, with the name of the competition stamped on them in gold. HAMPTON CLASSIC JUNIOR HUNTER GRAND CHAMPION, Nate read. "Cool," he said handing back the ribbons. He wished he'd found that joint.

"Check this out." Georgie pulled a large white plastic canister out of the trunk and placed it in Nate's hands.

The canister rattled as Nate turned it over. The name of an equine veterinary practice was printed on one side. *Connecticut Equine Health.* He looked up at Georgie questioningly.

"They're horse tranquilizers. I've taken them before. Half a pill is enough to send you to another planet, I swear."

Nate noticed that there were tiny beads of sweat on her upper lip, which was strange, because the attic was unheated and he was freezing his ass off. He shrugged and handed the canister back, uninterested.

Georgie unscrewed the top and shook the giant white pills into her sweaty palm. "Come on. This time I'm taking a whole one. Or maybe we should each take two and see what happens." Her dark hair fell into her eyes and she shook it away impatiently as she counted out the pills.

Nate stared at her, feeling frightened all of a sudden. He was pretty sure Georgie had taken some kind of pill when she'd disappeared into her bathroom before, and she had already been baked before that, so adding a horse tranquilizer to the mix sounded like the worst idea he'd ever heard. What was he going to do with a totally fucked-up ODed girl in the attic of a huge mansion in Greenwich, Connecticut, in the middle of the worst snowstorm in New England history?

"I think I'll pass." He pointed to a little metal device in the trunk, thinking that maybe if he diverted her attention, Georgie would forget all about the pills. "What's that?"

"A hoof pick," she answered quickly, holding out the pills. "The groom uses it to clean out the horses' hooves. Come on, take one."

Nate shook his head, his mind fumbling for a way to get both of them out of the realm of horse pills and into safer territory.

"Georgie," he said looking into her dark brown eyes with his sparkling emerald green ones and grabbing her wrist hard so that the horse pills scattered on the floor. He swept her up in his arms and kissed her dark red lips. "Let's go back downstairs, okay?"

Georgie let her head fall heavily against his chest. "Okay," she demurred. Her dark, silky hair trailed almost to the floor as Nate carried her down the long hall from the attic stairs to her bedroom. He pulled back the plush white duvet and set her down on the bed, but she clung to him.

"Don't leave me alone."

Nate wasn't planning to. Who knew what she'd do if he did.

"I'll be back in a sec," he said, extracting himself. He walked across the room and into the bathroom, leaving the door ajar so he could catch Georgie before she did anything dumb. Lined up on the counter next to the bathroom sink were three little bottles of prescription pills. Nate recognized the name Percoset because he'd taken the painkiller when he'd had his wisdom teeth removed, but he didn't recognize the names of the other two. None of the three prescriptions were made out to Georgina Spark.

He washed his hands and then went back into the bedroom. Georgie lay flat on her stomach in her white cotton underwear, snoring softly and looking much more innocent than she deserved to. Nate sat down beside her and watched her for a while. The bones in her vertebrae stuck out from her back, moving up and down as she breathed. He wondered if he should call someone, or if it was normal for Georgie to just take a bunch of pills and then go to sleep.

In the Breakaway meeting that day Jackie had said that if they were ever struggling and needed a hand to reach out to, they could call her. Nate pulled his cell phone out of his pocket and searched for Jackie's number, which she'd insisted everyone program in during the meeting. Nate had thought there was no way he'd ever need it. He stood up and went back into the bathroom as the phone began to ring.

It rang for a long time before Jackie finally answered groggily. "Yes?"

Nate looked at his watch, realizing too late that it was two o'clock in the morning. "Hey," he said slowly. "This is Nate Archibald from your group that met today?" he explained, wishing he sounded less stoned. "I'm, um, at that girl Georgie's house? I just found out she took a whole bunch of pills and I think she's fine—she's sleeping—but I just wanted to ask you, you know, should I do something?"

"Nate," Jackie said urgently, suddenly sounding like she'd just drunk ten cups of coffee, "I want you to read me the labels on the pills, and, if you can, tell me how many she took."

Nate picked up the bottles and read out the names. He didn't mention the horse pills, but he was pretty sure Georgie hadn't ingested any of those. "I don't know how many," he said helplessly. "I wasn't watching when she took them."

"And you're sure she's asleep? Her breathing is regular? She's not vomiting or choking?"

Nate rushed into the bedroom feeling more alarmed than ever, but Georgie was still sleeping peaccfully, her ribs expanding and contracting gently with cach breath, her dark hair fanned out on the pillow around her head, looking exactly like a sleeping Snow White. "Yeah," he said, relieved. "She's sleeping."

"Okay. I want you to stay there and watch her. Just make sure she doesn't start to vomit, and if she docs, sit her up, lean her over your shoulder and pat her on the back so she doesn't choke on it. I know it sounds unpleasant, but you want her to be well. You want to facilitate her recovery."

"Okay," Nate answered shakily. He glanced at Georgie again, praying she wouldn't do anything weird.

"I'm going to send a van over from the clinic. It's going to be a while because the roads are basically closed, but I don't think you're too far away—they'll make it there eventually. Are you prepared to stay strong, Nate? Remember, you're our hero tonight, our Prince Charming, our knight in shining armor."

Nate walked over to the bedroom window and peered out. There was so much snow, the circular gravel driveway in front of the mansion was indistinguishable from the vast lawns beyond. He didn't feel like Prince Charming—he felt helpless and trapped, like Rapunzel. Hadn't he been in enough trouble already? "Okay," he told Jackie, trying to sound more confident than he felt. "I'll see you soon." He hung up his phone and stuffed it into his back pocket.

Of course our Prince Charming was completely unaware that he might have just saved Snow White's life. But it's the reluctant heroes of fairy tales that we fall in love with over and over, despite their flaws.

gossipgirl.net

topics ◀ *previous* *next* ▶ *post a question* *reply*

Disclaimer: All the real names of places, people, and events have been altered or abbreviated to protect the innocent. Namely, me.

hey people!

Do we really need to look like Little Red Riding Hood?

Every Fashion Week I find myself asking, Why are all the models in the shows wearing space suits, or dressed like Hansel and Gretel, or basically naked, when I wouldn't be caught dead looking like that on the street? Then I have to remind myself that the shows are really a spectacle and that the whole point of fashion is to entertain and spark the imagination and make the world a better place. Fashion is art, and art imitates life; there's no reason to it. The more I think about it, the more I can't wait to dress up like Little Red Riding Hood myself and prowl around looking for wolves. Time to shop for a red cape!

What happened to all that snow?!

How come whenever there's a serious snowstorm in the city, it only takes a few hours for the snow to melt off the sidewalks and then everything is back to normal again, just in time for school on Monday? I think it's a plot to ensure that we all have to go to school on Valentine's Day, which should totally be a national no-school holiday. I think I'm going to take the day off anyway. How else am I going to enjoy the roses, chocolates, and jewelry I'm going to get from my secret admirers?

Your e-mail

Dear GG,
I'm bummed that this girl I like maybe doesn't like me in the same way. Your site cheers me up.
—blue

A: Hey blue,
How do you know she doesn't like you? Have you asked her? Remember, though, I'm always here for you when that girl lets you down.
—GG

Q: dear gg,
you are hot. will you be my valentine?
—oskar

A: Dear oskar,
Thank you for the compliment. Unfortunately I'm already spoken for, and I have an extremely hot evening planned. But if you still want to shower me with gifts, I definitely won't complain.
—GG

Sightings

B leaving a downtown hotel alone Friday late night and taking the *subway* uptown, of all shockingly pedestrian things. Guess that's one place she thought she wouldn't be spotted. *Wrong.* **S, Les Best's Chief d'Affairs,** and **Les Best** himself, wearing his signature black ski suit, outside the offices of the **Little Hearts** children's charity early yesterday morning, looking like they'd been up all night. Serena was wearing a pink bra and some guy's ski jacket. Whatever happened to her boyfriend? **N** arriving at **Grand Central** yesterday afternoon, looking dazed and confused but still gorgeous, of course. **D** stumbling out of a cab and into **Agnès B. Homme** to shop. Wait, are we talking about the same **D**? I guess **Agnès B.** is French, and he always fancied himself an existentialist, which is a French concept, but wait—I digress. **V** filming a bullterrier trailing yellow pee behind it in the white snow. Well, it's nice to know *she* hasn't changed.

May your Valentine's Day be filled with adoration, pampering, and a pair of gorgeous, tiny-heeled Jimmy Choo sandals that are completely useless in this weather. Just remember: You are totally worth it.

You know you love me.

gossip girl

the icing on b's cake

All Monday morning Blair had been dreading peer group. Not that she minded talking about hooking up with boys, or peer pressure, or whatever else the freshmen wanted to talk about. After all, today was Valentine's Day, so *everyone* at Constance was talking about hooking up with boys. What she dreaded were all the questions the ninth graders in the group were going to ask Serena about walking the runway in the Les Best show, what it had been like to hang out with all those famous models, and blah, blah, blah. They'd probably ask about her stupid I LOVE AARON T-shirt and what was going on with her and Aaron, because *they'd* heard blah, blah, blah. As if it was all so very interesting.

Not.

Why was it that the world was so full of followers when there were so many choices in life? Blair slipped an extra slice of chocolate cake onto her tray just to make sure she'd have something to do while the girls in peer group were boring her to death.

"Hello," she practically yawned when she sat down at the crowded table a few minutes after the group had begun. "Sorry I'm late."

"That's okay," Serena replied gaily. She'd gotten a complimentary trim and highlight job before the fashion show, and her long blond hair was even shinier and more perfect than it had been before. "We were just talking about Elise's parental problems. She thinks her dad might be having an affair."

Elise's thick, straw-colored bangs were pulled back and clipped to the sides of her head with tiny pink heart barrettes. There were dark circles under her bright blue eyes, like she'd been up all night worrying. "That sucks," Blair said sympathetically. "Believe me, I *know*." She decided to leave it at that. Peer group might have been a place for sharing, but she wasn't about to go into the details of her father's affairs with other men while he was still married to her mother.

Serena nodded vigorously. "I was just telling them how all families are totally fucked up. Actually, Blair, your family is a perfect example," she added cheerfully.

Blair bristled. "Thanks a lot," she shot back. "But I don't think everyone needs to hear about my problems right now."

Jenny bit a cuticle and banged her foot nervously against the leg of her chair. She'd been fretting all morning that as soon as peer group started, Elise was going to dive right in and start talking about same-sex kissing. Thank God Elise had other things on her mind.

"Anyway, we don't have to talk about our messed-up families if it's going bother you," Blair told Elise, trying to be supportive.

Elise nodded unhappily. "Actually there *was* something else I wanted to talk about."

Jenny winced.

Oops.

Blair nodded encouragingly, "Yes? What is it?"

Vicky Reinerson waved her hand in the air. She was wearing

a red wool cape similar to the one Serena had modeled in the Les Best show, except hers was a little used looking, like she'd borrowed it from her grandmother or something.

Guess she didn't get the message that capes are back in style this *fall*, not this spring.

"Oh, but after she's done will you *please* tell us all about the Les Best show, Serena?" Vicky pleaded. "You *promised*."

Serena giggled as if she had *tons* of crazy stories to tell. Blair wanted to smack her. "The craziest thing was that I had a snowball fight with Les Best himself and I didn't even know it was him!" Serena glanced at Blair, who was glaring at her. "Anyway, I'll save it for the end, if there's time." She turned back to Elise. "What was it you were saying?"

Elise's face turned purple as a plum. "I-I wanted to talk about kissing," she stammered. "About kissing *girls*."

Jenny kicked the legs of Elise's chair. Mary, Cassie, and Vicky snickered and nudged each other's elbows. This was going to be good. A rumor had gone around awhile back that Blair and Serena had kissed each other in the hot tub in the hotel suite Chuck Bass's family kept downtown in the Tribeca Star.

"I think anyone should be able to kiss anyone," Serena replied. "Kissing is fun!"

Blair forked a giant piece of chocolate cake into her mouth, trying to come up with something to top what Serena had just said. "Guys like to watch girls kiss," she declared with her mouth full. "They do it all the time in the movies, just to turn guys on." This was true. They'd even talked about it in Mr. Beckham's film class.

"So Serena, what *was* it like to wear all those cool Les Best clothes?" Jenny asked, desperate to change the subject.

Serena stretched her long, lithe arms over her gorgeous blond head and sighed happily. "You really want to know?"

Everyone in the group except Blair and Elise nodded eagerly. "Okay, I'll tell you."

Blair rolled her eyes, daring herself to shut Serena up by announcing the news of her torrid affair with a married thirty-eight-year-old man, which was a hell of a lot more interesting than prancing around on a runway in dumb clothes no one wanted to wear anyway. She glanced down at the table where Elise was furiously scribbling her name over and over on a sheet of notebook paper. *Elise Wells. Miss Elise Wells. Miss Elise Patricia Wells. E. P. Wells.*

Suddenly Blair felt the entire contents of her stomach do a back walkover into her throat. *Wells?* That was *Owen*'s last name. And Elise had just said she thought her *father* was having an *affair*. Owen hadn't said anything to her about a daughter, but now that she thought about it, Elise had his same eyes, and on the stoop Elise had lit two cigarettes exactly the same way Owen had Friday night in the bar. *Christ.* For all Blair knew, Owen had *ten* children that he'd just happened to forget to mention. *Fuck!*

Blair scraped her chair back and bolted for the nurse's office behind the cafeteria, getting there just in time to spew chocolate cake all over Nurse O'Donnell's hand-hooked farmhouse rug. It wasn't pretty, but it was the quickest way to get sent home sick from school.

As soon as she left, the cafeteria began to hum with the sound of girls trading versions of what was wrong with Blair Waldorf.

"I heard she has some rare disease. She lost all her hair. That's really a wig," announced Laura Salmon.

"I heard she's pregnant with some old guy's kid. He's married to a member of the royal family and he wants to marry her, but his wife won't give him a divorce," Rain Hoffstetter explained.

"Oh my God. So she and her mom could like, have babies at the same time!" Kati Farkas shrieked.

"She's not pregnant, stupid. It's her eating disorder," Isabel Coates told the girls at the same table in a confidential whisper. "She's been struggling with it for years."

At the peer group table, Serena unwittingly set the record straight. "She'll be *fine* just as soon as she finds out she's into Yale."

apathy vs. poetry

"Happy Valentine's Day, loverboy," Zeke Freedman greeted Dan as fourth-period U.S. history was about to begin. He handed Dan a pink paper shopping bag. "Aggie asked me to give this to you. A messenger just brought it to the front desk."

The handles of the bag were tied with red satin ribbon. Dan tugged on the bow and emptied the contents of the bag out onto his desk: a small white box and a slim red leather book. Inside the white box was a stubby silver pen on a silver chain. A card inside the box described it as an antigravity pen, the kind used by astronauts in space. Dan put the chain around his neck and opened the leather book up to the first page where someone had scrawled a note: *Kick gravity's ass, you charmer. Dig?*

Dan reread the note, completely dumbfounded. It was too bizarre for Vanessa, which meant it was definitely from Mystery. The final bell rang and Mr. Dube strode into the room and started erasing the blackboard. Dan tucked the bag of presents under his seat and opened his notebook, pretending to listen to what Mr. Dube was saying about Vietnam and apathy. School seemed so lame and inconsequential when a big-time agent like Rusty Klein wanted to represent him, and an obviously brilliant, intriguingly sexy poet had sent him those exquisitely astute Valentine's Day gifts.

Then Dan remembered Vanessa and his hands began to tremble. He hadn't sent her anything for Valentine's Day—not that Vanessa was at all into such a "commercial bullshit holiday," as she called it, but he hadn't even called her. Actually, his biggest problem was . . . he'd cheated on her. And not just kissing cheating either. *Cheating* cheating.

Whoops.

It was all Mystery's fault. With her see-through slip and crooked yellow teeth she'd made him feel like he was living inside of one of his poems, kissing a beguilingly odd girl he'd created at a raucous, screwball party he'd invented. He hadn't been able to help but let his imagination run amok, sending him stumbling across the snowy landscape to her ramshackle Chinatown studio apartment and making love to her in all sorts of odd yogalike positions on her uncomfortable futon bed as the sun was rising over the bleak, snow-covered city. It was almost as if none of it had actually *happened*. It was *fiction*.

Except it wasn't fiction. He'd cheated.

Dan had been dreadfully hungover for the remainder of the weekend and too deeply mired in existential guilt and self-loathing to answer Vanessa's countless messages on his cell phone.

He flipped to the back of his history notebook. What if he wrote Vanessa a poem and e-mailed it to her during lunch next period? That would be more meaningful than flowers or chocolate or a cheesy Valentine's Day card. The best thing about it was that he wouldn't have to talk to her and possibly admit that he'd cheated on her, because he'd never been any good at telling lies.

Mr. Dube was writing on the board now. Dan pretended to makes notes in his notebook.

Chalk angels, he wrote. *Making meaning.*

Then he thought about something Mystery had said when they were drinking their fourth or fifth Red Bull cocktails. Something about how she was tired of writing obscure poems that skirted around what she was really trying to say. Subtle was out. Direct was in.

Kiss me. Be mine. Dan wrote, imitating the little slogans on those candy hearts girls were always passing around on Valentine's Day. *Hot stuff!*

He reread the words without really seeing them. His mind was still too full of his night with Mystery to process anything else. Her stringy dirty blond hair had smelled like toast and when she'd touched his bare stomach with her cold, clammy hands, his whole body had rippled. He'd never even asked her what she meant by premature death or how his poem "Sluts" had saved her life, but he'd been so intoxicated by the taurine in the Red Bull and by her appallingly yellow teeth, he probably wouldn't have remembered anyway.

Lost my virginity again, Dan wrote, which was the truth. Doing it with Mystery was like losing it again. Was it possible that every time he made love to a new woman it would feel that way?

Before he could imagine who the next lucky girl would be, the bell rang and Dan snapped out of his reverie, slapping the notebook closed and tucking it under his arm. "Hey," he called to Zeke. "I'll buy you some sushi for lunch if you wait for me to whip off an e-mail in the lab."

"Okay." Zeke shrugged, trying not to look too excited that his old friend was actually deigning to pay attention to him again. Since when did Dan Humphrey, king of cheap egg rolls and bad coffee, eat *sushi*?

"Heard you got lucky Friday night!" Chuck Bass shouted Dan's way as they passed each other on the stairwell. Chuck was wearing his Riverside Prep uniform navy blue V-neck sweater with nothing on underneath it. "Nice work."

"Thanks," Dan muttered, hurrying upstairs to the computer lab. He was kidding himself if he thought Vanessa wasn't going to find out about him and Mystery, but as soon as she received his latest poem he was convinced she'd forgive him. Just as Mystery had written in her note—he was a charmer.

girls go gaga over secret admirers

Vanessa felt a little ridiculous hanging out with the desperate girls in the packed, overheated Constance Billard computer lab, all checking their e-mail for the hundredth time to see who'd sent them a pathetic e-card for Valentine's Day or posted a message on their Secret Admirer page, the alarmingly uncreative new tradition the school had started last Valentine's Day. But Dan usually logged on at least once a day, and since he'd been so busy this weekend meeting Rusty Klein at the Better Than Naked show and hadn't had a chance to call her back all weekend, she figured he might try to e-mail her today, especially since it was Valentine's Day— not that either of them really bought into that commercial holiday bullshit.

Of course not.

"Hey," she heard someone say. It was Dan's little sister, checking out her Secret Admirer page at the next terminal.

"Hey Jennifer."

Jenny rolled herself backwards on her black swivel chair and then pulled herself forward again. Her curly brown hair was blow-dried straight and she looked older and more sophisticated than usual. "So you and Dan must have had fun at that fashion show. He didn't get home until like, Saturday afternoon. My dad was grumbling about how spoiled and irresponsible we both are, but then he completely forgot to yell at Dan. As usual."

Vanessa smoothed her hand over her practically shaved head. "Actually, I didn't go to the same show he went to. I got invited to another one."

Jenny looked confused. "Oh."

In the back of her mind Vanessa sensed that something was wrong. What had Dan been doing out all that time anyway? But then again, everything had gotten screwed up in the snow. Maybe he'd spent the night at Zeke's house or something. Zeke lived downtown.

She logged on as hairlesscat, password *meow*, and clicked on her inbox. Sure enough, there was a message from Dan, and—big surprise—it was a poem. Vanessa read the poem eagerly, grimacing when she recognized that Dan had put absolutely no effort into it at all. *Hot stuff?* What was that all about? And what was up with *"I lost my virginity again"*? Who was he fucking kidding?

She hit reply and wrote back: *Ha ha. I laughed. I cried. What's your deal anyway? We're supposed to be making a film together, remember?*

As she waited for Dan to respond, she logged onto her Secret Admirer page. To her surprise there were four messages:

```
I can't stop raving about you to all my
boyfriends. No one mixes form with meaning
the way you do, milady. —prettyboy

You give this fucked-up world a new kind
of beauty. Keep your freak on. —d.
```

Happy Valentine's Day to my very special
sister on a special day. ——RubyTuesday

Can you make it to Cannes? Let's talk over
coffee in Brooklyn Thurs. eve? ——the filmmaker who discovered you

Vanessa rolled her eyes as she read the last one. She
appreciated everything Ken Mogul had done for her, but he
hadn't exactly discovered her. She'd been there all along.

She clicked on her inbox again but there was no response
from Dan so she logged off. "See you later," she whispered to
Jenny, whose big brown eyes were glued to her computer.

"See you," Jenny replied without looking up. There were
three whole messages on her Secret Admirer page.

sorry i didn't get you any candy but i
wasn't sure which kind you like. let's get
some after school. don't really feel like
going home right away anyway. ——sadgirl

btw, when do you want to finish that
painting?? ——me again

Those two were very definitely from Elise, but the third one
sounded like it might very well be from a genuine, real-life *boy*.

Sorry it took me so long, but I didn't have
the guts to write to you before. If you
want to meet me, I take the Seventy-ninth
Street crosstown bus home after school. I'm
not sure what you look like, but if you see

a really tall skinny guy with blond hair
looking at you on the bus, smile because
it's probably me. Happy Valentine's Day,
JHumphrey. Can't wait to meet you. Love, L

Jenny reread the message over and over. A tall skinny guy with blond hair? He sounded exactly like the boy she'd seen in Bendel's! But what did *L* stand for? Lester? Lance? Louis? No, those names sounded too geeky, and his message didn't sound geeky at all, just sweet. But how had he gotten her e-mail address? Oh, who cared—she couldn't believe it: *he wanted to meet her!!*

Jenny immediately deleted Elise's messages and ran to the printer to retrieve the one from L. Of course, she planned to ride the Seventy-ninth Street crosstown bus all afternoon and all night if that was what it took. But, God forbid, if they never found each other, Jenny would have his love note to cherish and keep forever and ever.

And she'd thought she was through with love. See how magical Valentine's Day can be?

hugs, not drugs

"So how come you didn't call 911?" Jeremy Scott Tompkinson asked Nate as he crumbled pot into the EZ Wider rolling paper spread out on his right knee.

"Give the dude a break," noted Charlie Dern. "He was stoned, remember?"

"I would've been like, 'See ya later, you crazy fucking chick! I don't care if you're putting out!'" quipped Anthony Avuldsen.

Jeremy had managed to steal some pot from his older brother who was home visiting from college, and now the four boys were huddled on a remote stoop on East End Avenue, taking a break before gym class.

Nate blew on his bare hands and stuffed them into his cashmere-lined coat pockets. "I don't know." He still felt pretty confused about it himself. "I guess I just wanted to call someone who knew us both. Someone I could trust."

Jeremy shook his head. "Dude, that's exactly what those rehab headshrinkers *want* you to do. They've got you programmed already."

Nate thought about the way Georgie imitated Jackie's corny psychobabble—all that stuff about healing wounds and negative friendships. It didn't seem like Georgie had been programmed. All of a sudden he wondered if she was angry that he'd called Jackie, but it wasn't like he could call her and ask her. She was now staying at Breakaway full time and wasn't allowed to take any phone calls, just in case one of her dealers called or something. Hopefully Nate would still see her in group.

"How long do you have to deal with that rehab bullshit anyway?" Charlie asked. He reached for the burning joint and took a hit.

"Six months," Nate answered. "But at least I don't have to live there." The other boys intoned bored and sympathetic sighs of disgust. Nate didn't say anything. Although he'd never have admitted it, he kind of liked going to rehab and meeting the different kids in group, especially Georgie. He'd be sort of sad when it was over.

"'Ere," Charlie said, passing Nate the joint.

Nate looked at it and shook his head. "No thanks," he murmured under his breath. There was a crushed red paper heart lying on the sidewalk in front of the stoop where the four boys were sitting. "Is it Valentine's Day?" he asked distractedly.

"Yeah," Anthony responded. "Why?"

"Huh," Nate replied. He stood up and brushed the snow off the back of his black Hugo Boss coat. For what seemed like forever he'd always sent a special girl roses on Valentine's Day. "I gotta go do something. Catch you guys in gym, okay?"

His friends watched him trudge purposefully through the slush toward Madison Avenue until he was out of sight. Something was happening to their old friend Nate Archibald, and it wasn't just that he'd turned down a joint for the first time since he was ten years old

Could it be, was it possible, that he'd fallen in love?

v-day turned d-day for b

Blair kept her hand clapped over her mouth and her mind clear of any thoughts of Owen the whole way home to keep from being sick all over the back seat of the taxi. But when she stepped off the wood-paneled elevator and into the penthouse, her nostrils were bombarded with the putrid scent of roses, causing her stomach to churn ominously once more. The entire front hall was packed with them. Yellow roses, white roses, pink ones and red. She dropped her bag on the floor and read the notes on the bouquets.

A—You're my honey-pie. Love, S, said the note on the yellow roses.

Audrey, my favorite little aristocrat, will you please be my Valentine? Love, Cary, said the note on the red roses.

My darling Mrs. Rose, May our tiny daughter be as lovely and as wonderful as you are and as hopelessly happy as I am every day I spend with you. —Your loving husband, Mr. Rose, said the note on the pink-and-white bouquet.

As if one of those notes wouldn't have been enough to make Blair puke out her already puked-out guts, she had to be bombarded with *three* uniquely repulsive missives. Throwing her coat down on the floor, she staggered into the nearest bathroom to empty her stomach again. "Mom!" she shouted, wiping her mouth on a parchment-colored *R*-monogrammed guest towel.

"Blair?" her mother called back. Eleanor Waldorf wandered slowly down the hall wearing a pink boiled wool Chanel suit that had been let out at the waist to accommodate her five-months pregnant belly. Her highlighted blond bob was pulled back into a neat ponytail and she was wearing white rabbit fur slippers and carrying her portable phone. Like most Upper East Side hostesses, Eleanor spent all the time she wasn't having lunch or getting her hair done on the phone. "What are you doing home?" she asked her daughter. "Are you sick?"

Blair clutched her stomach and tried not to look at her mother. "I saw the note from Cyrus," she croaked. "You're having a girl?"

Her mother beamed back at her, her blue eyes sparkling ecstatically. "Isn't it wonderful?" she cried. "I found out this morning." She flip-flopped up to Blair in her fur slippers and threw her arms around her daughter's neck. "Cyrus has always wanted a girl. And now when you come home from college you'll have a little baby sister to play with!"

Blair grimaced as her stomach did another back flip at the mention of college.

"I hope you don't mind," Eleanor babbled on. "But we're planning to turn your room into a nursery since we're running out of bedrooms. You and Aaron will be going away to school soon anyway. You don't mind, do you, sweetheart?"

Blair stared at her mother blankly. She hadn't wanted a stepbrother or a stepfather and she certainly didn't want a baby sister, especially not one who was going to take over her *room*. "I'm going to go lie down," she replied weakly.

"I'll have Myrtle send in some bouillon," her mother called after her.

Blair slammed her bedroom door and dove onto her bed, burying her head in the depths of her extrasoft goose-down pillows. Kitty Minky, her gray Russian Blue cat, jumped onto her back and kneaded his paws into her black-and-white Fair Isle sweater. "Help me," Blair moaned miserably to her cat. If only she could lie there until late August and then be helicoptered to her new dorm room at Yale, skipping all the bad parts in the script of the movie that was her life, the parts that needed to be rewritten.

Out of habit, she reached out and punched the playback button on the answering machine on her bedside table, keeping her eyes closed as she listened.

"Hello, Blair, it's Owen. Owen Wells. Sorry I couldn't call earlier. What happened? I woke up and you were gone. Anyway, Happy Valentine's Day, gorgeous. Call me back when you have a moment. Bye-bye."

"Hello, Blair, it's Owen again. Did you get my flowers? I hope you like them. Call me back when you have a moment. Thanks. 'Bye."

"Hello, Blair. I know it's short notice, but would you like to have dinner with me? Um, this is Owen by the way. Plans on the home front have changed and I'm all freed up. So how 'bout Le Cirque this evening, gorgeous? Give me a call."

"Hello, Blair. I got a table at Le Cirque—" Blair kicked her answering machine off the bedside table and it came unplugged. She didn't care that Owen had the sexiest voice and was the best kisser in all of New York. She couldn't play Audrey to his Cary anymore, not when Cary had turned out to be a lying, cheating, son-of-a-bitch, scumbag *dad*. She didn't even care if Owen told Yale she was a stupid flake who wouldn't last more than two weeks there. Fuck Owen, and fuck Yale.

She grabbed her phone and dialed Owen's cell phone number. It was the only number he'd given her, probably because it was the only phone he could be sure of answering himself.

"Blair?" Owen answered eagerly on the first ring. "Where have you been? I've been trying to get ahold of you all day!"

"In high school?" Blair shot back. "I know it was a long time ago for you, but it's this place where you go during the week where they teach you stuff. I'm only home now because I'm not feeling well."

"Oh. I guess you're not up for dinner then?"

Owen's voice didn't sound nearly as sexy now that she knew what a complete asshole he was. Blair walked over to the full-length mirror on the back of her closet door and examined her hair. It already looked a little longer. Maybe it wouldn't take that long to grow back. Or maybe she'd cut it even shorter. She pulled her hair back severely from her forehead to see what it would look like supershort.

"I know your daughter," she hissed into the phone as she walked over to her dresser and dug around in the top drawer until she found the little pair of silver antique sewing scissors she'd inherited from her grandmother and never had much use for.

"B-Blair—," Owen stammered.

"Fuck off." Blair clicked off the phone and threw it onto her bed. Then, grabbing a handful of hair, she began to hack away with the tiny silver sewing scissors.

Good-bye, Audrey Hepburn, hello Mia Farrow in *Rosemary's Baby*!

gossipgirl.net

hey people!

The least painful way to say good-bye

Sad but true, the reality of Valentine's Day is that it makes demands on relationships that those relationships may not be able to handle. What do you do when you both know it's over and you just want to move on so you can start maxing out your credit cards on presents for yourself instead of for someone else? In my vast experience with painless breakups, the less you say the better. Don't hash things out. A simple gesture means so much more. An invitation to do something 'with the gang' instead of alone together. A tender kiss on the cheek. A good-bye wave. And don't you dare return any gifts. They're yours! Keep 'em.

One thing you may not have realized about me

I *am* real. That means I have a birthday. Next Monday I turn eighteen and I'm having a party and you're all invited. I know what you're thinking, it's *Monday*. But really, what else have you got to do on a Monday night? Your Latin homework? A do-it-yourself facial? Plus, the week will *fly* by afterwards, I promise.
When? Monday, 9 P.M. till dawn.
Where? Gnome. Don't worry if you've never heard of it. No one has. It's a brand-spanking-new club on Bond Street celebrating its opening night with my party. Isn't that sweet?
What to bring? Yourself, your most beautiful friends, and of course, *a present*!

Sightings

B absent from school for the second day in a row. **D** waiting around in the lobby of the **Plaza Hotel** looking nervous in his spiffy new Agnès B.

suit. **S** at the **Les Best** atelier trying on a gorgeous sunflower yellow dress for a photo shoot. **J** riding the Seventy-ninth Street crosstown bus back and forth through the park for *hours*. **A** playing guitar on the train back from Scarsdale, where he's been hiding out for days. **N** jogging around Central Park—so much clean living gives a boy energy!

Your e-mail

Dear Gossip Girl,
I kissed a girl (I'm a girl too) but I didn't mean anything by it. Actually, there's a boy I like. What should I say to this girl without hurting her feelings, because she's my friend?
—doubletrouble

Dear double,
I've never been a big believer in the theory that kissing someone is a promise you won't kiss anyone else. Kissing is fun. Why limit yourself to just one kissee? The trick is telling the person you're just having fun, you're not planning to get married or anything. BTW, it's best to do this *before* you kiss them, not after.
—GG

Dear GG,
I'm stuck in rehab and I'm allowed to log onto the Web but certain e-mail accounts are blocked so I can't send a message to this boy I'm hung up on and miss so much. He even sent me roses! Luckily I can get on your site so I can tell the world that I'm in love. Maybe when I get out of here we can have a drink to celebrate. It's on me.
—rehab babe

Dear babe,
Instead of us having a drink when you get out, you should start a site of your own. Or write a book. Just a suggestion.
—GG

Don't forget my party—wish list to come!

You know you love me.

gossip girl

lifestyles of the rich and famous

Wednesday after school Dan stood in the lobby of the Plaza Hotel, fiddling with the collar of his new black Agnès B. suit jacket and clutching the small red leather-bound book Mystery had given him for Valentine's Day. He'd been to the Plaza only once before, when he and Vanessa had been in Central Park filming ice skaters and she'd had to use the bathroom. Even in his fancy new suit he felt out of place in such sumptuous surroundings.

He'd better get used to it. After all, he was about to become a very famous author who had tea with his agent in fancy hotels on a regular basis.

Pauper in a mirrored castle, he thought, forming the beginnings of a poem.

"Daniel!" Dan heard Rusty Klein shout from across the room. This time she was wearing her red wig in fat braids on either side of her head, and her immense, six-foot-plus frame was cloaked in an unusual black Japanese geisha robe dotted with tiny white flowers and paired with tall, black suede stiletto boots—as if she wasn't already tall enough. Mystery stood at her side looking like a starved ghost in a tattered plum-colored wrap dress and worn brown leather boots. Her collarbone stuck out from her skinny frame like an airplane wing, and her lips were so chapped, they were completely white.

Skeleton princess drifts out on a ray of dust.

"Hey," Dan greeted them casually, as if he always hung out at the Plaza after school. Inside his white Agnès B. shirt the silver gravity pen Mystery had given him beat against his pale chest. "Thank you for the gifts."

Rusty swept him up in a big bear hug, suffocating him with her rank oily-fish perfume and smudging his cheek with orangey-pink lipstick. "Mystery and I had *too* much fun shopping for you, darling! We had to *force* ourselves to stop."

Mystery ran her tongue over her yellow teeth. "We've been drinking martinis and deconstructing Kafka like two old ninnies," she croaked, sounding drunk and looking like she hadn't slept in weeks. She blinked her sleepy gray eyes. "Now that you're here I can eat. You starve me."

Bones draped in moth wings sewn with cobwebs.

"This way," Rusty chortled, ignoring Mystery's odd pronouncement. She ushered them through the immense lobby and into a large tearoom full of gilded mirrors, tinkling crystal, and overly perfumed ladies with freshly blown-out hair. The round, white-clothed table had been laid with a silver tea service and a three-tiered silver tray covered with freshly baked scones, pots of homemade jam, and tiny cucumber sandwiches with the crusts cut off. Two half-empty martini glasses stood on the table, ready to be polished off.

"We've been having a little party to celebrate Mystery's debut," Rusty explained merrily. She sat down and tossed back the remains of her drink.

The queen of poesy gives a tempting tug.

Dan sat down next to her and put his red leather book on the table. "What debut?"

Rusty grabbed a blueberry scone and slathered it with butter, shoving the whole thing into her enormous orangey-pink mouth, where it disappeared instantly. "Good, you brought your observations book. Have you been writing everything down? Remember, nothing is inconsequential!" She winked at Mystery. "Who knows? It could all add up to a book!"

Mystery giggled and glanced at Dan. "I finished my novel," she confided huskily.

House on fire! House on fire!

Dan rubbed his thumb over the tines of his fork, as he absorbed the information. Mystery had finished writing an entire novel in less than a week and all he'd done was write one crappy Valentine's Day poem for Vanessa. He couldn't even bear to read Vanessa's response after he'd sent the poem to her, that was how badly it sucked.

"But I thought you'd just started it," he said, feeling weirdly betrayed.

"I had. But Sunday night I fell off the plateau and kept gathering momentum, and I just couldn't stop writing until I finished. I e-mailed it to Rusty at dawn this morning, just as the street cleaners were arriving. She's already read the whole thing. She says I'm the next Virginia Woolf!"

"I thought you were the next Sylvia Plath," Dan accused grumpily.

Moth princess helps herself to stolen meat.

Mystery shrugged her thin shoulders and poured a heaping spoonful of sugar into her martini, stirring it pensively before picking up the glass with both hands and taking a gulp.

"Anyhoo, let's talk about *you* Dannyboy," Rusty practically shouted. "Oh, fuck me." She pulled her hot pink cell phone out of her purse, pushed a few buttons and held it up to her ear. "Hold on, loves. I have to call my messages."

Dan waited, watching Mystery dunk so many spoonfuls of sugar into her drink that it looked less like a martini and more like a slushy from 7-Eleven. He hadn't noticed before, but her gnarly, gnawed-on fingernails were as yellow as her teeth.

Rusty tossed her cell phone into the middle of the table. "I think you should write a memoir," she told Dan, reaching for another scone and breaking it in half. "*Memoir of a Young Poet.* I love it!" she shouted. "You're the next Rilke!"

The queen of clowns pulls a pink rabbit out of her hair.

Dan tugged on the gravity pen. He wanted to write down something about Mystery's yellow fingernails in his observation book and how surprising it was that he wasn't turned off by them. In fact, they turned him *on*.

"But how can I write a memoir when all I do is go to high school?" he argued miserably. "Nothing big has ever happened to me." He reached for the teapot with trembling hands and poured warm, fragrant Earl Grey tea into his white teacup. Ah, *caffeine*.

Rusty tapped the cover of his observation book with her long, orangey-pink fingernails. "*Small things*, darling. Small things. And you might want to think about putting off college and writing for a year or two, just like Mystery." She wiped her mouth with a white cloth napkin, smearing it with lipstick. "I've got you signed up with Mystery for a poetry reading at the Rivington Rover Poetry Club tomorrow night. Buckley is already distributing the flyers. It's very now. All the old poetry clubs are coming back. You've got to be able to perform. I'm telling you, poetry is the next rock'n'roll!"

Mystery giggled and kicked Dan's shin under the table like drunken donkey. Dan was tempted to kick her back because it kind of hurt, but he didn't want to be immature.

Rusty snapped her foot-long fingers and the waiter

instantly appeared. "Give these kids anything their little hearts desire," she directed. "I have to run, darlings. Mama has a meeting." She blew kisses at them and then click-clacked across the room in her geisha dress, turning heads with her flaming braids and immense stature.

Mother bird flees the nest, leaving the princess and the pauper with open beaks.

Mystery downed the dregs of Rusty's martini and gazed exhaustedly at Dan with droopy gray eyes. "Every time Rusty mentions your name I feel the heat creep up my thighs," she confessed throatily. "I've been drowning in desire all week, but I managed to channel that animal energy into my book." She giggled. Her teeth looked like they'd been colored in with a yellow crayon. "Parts of it are totally X-rated."

Pauper turns prince. To coin a phrase, I'm crowning.

Dan reached for a cucumber sandwich and shoved it in his mouth, chewing it violently without even tasting it. He was supposed to go home and write his memoir. He was supposed to have a girlfriend. He was supposed to be freaked out by this decidedly insane, yellow-toothed, horny chick. But the truth was, he was horny, too. He'd lost his virginity twice already, and he couldn't wait to lose it again and again.

"Come on," Mystery beckoned, holding out her yellow-nailed hand. "We can get a room and put it on Rusty's tab."

Dan picked up his observation book and followed her to the front desk. Poetry be damned. He couldn't resist following this story line to the next chapter.

I is for love

Jenny couldn't be sure that the L who'd sent her a note on Valentine's Day was actually the boy from Bendel's. He could've been a total nerd or even a gross, perverted old man, but secretly she was already in love with him. She felt like a girl in a fairy tale in love with a man in a mask, and she was determined to ride the Seventy-ninth Street crosstown bus until she met him face-to-face. Monday and Tuesday she rode the bus alone until 7 P.M. with no luck. On Wednesday after school Elise came with her.

"I don't get it. Why are we doing this again?" Elise asked. She'd already finished all her homework and was staring out the window over Jenny's shoulder, bored nearly to tears.

"I told you. I left my favorite hat on the bus this morning and if I ride enough buses, I'm sure I'll see it," Jenny lied.

"Someone probably took it," Elise argued. "Your cute fuzzy red hat? I'm sure someone took it."

A swollen-ankled middle-aged woman wearing a dowdy trench coat and reading the *Wall Street Journal* glared at them the way people are always glaring at teenagers when they're talking in public. Like, could you please just press the mute button? Well, *excuse* me.

"Just this last bus and then we can go home," Jenny promised, even though she'd promised that two buses ago.

Elise put her hand on Jenny's black-stockinged knee and left it there. "I don't really mind. It's not like I have anything better to do."

Jenny waited for Elise to remove her hand. "What are you doing?" she whispered loudly.

"With what?"

"With your *hand*."

"The book says to express your affection with gentle caresses," Elise declared.

"But I don't want you to. Besides, we're on a *bus*," Jenny hissed, pushing Elise's hand away. The last thing she wanted was for L to see her and Elise *caressing* each other. *God.* How embarrassing.

"What's wrong with it?" Elise cried, shoving Jenny in the leg just as the bus lurched over a bump. Jenny slipped off the seat and onto the floor, her butt landing hard on her neighbor's shoes.

Jenny closed her eyes, too mortified to open them. If her secret admirer were watching now, he wouldn't be writing her any more love notes. The bus lurched over another bump as it roared across the park and Jenny's boobs bounced mercilessly, as if she hadn't been through enough.

"Here." A hand gripped her arm.

"Fuck off," Jenny mumbled in total humiliation. She batted the hand away and struggled to her feet. A blond head loomed above her. Tall. Nice nose. Hazel eyes with blond-tipped lashes. It was *him*—the Bendel's boy!

"Are you all right?" he asked. "There's an empty seat back here. Why don't you sit down?" He took her hand and pushed backward through the crowd.

Jenny slid into the hard, narrow seat and looked up at the boy, her heart pounding. He looked to be about sixteen and he was perfect, just perfect. "Are you L?" she asked breathlessly.

He smiled shyly. One of his front teeth was chipped a little. It was extremely cute. "Yes. It's Leo," he answered.

Leo. Of course.

"I'm Jennifer!" Jenny practically screamed, she was so excited.

"Jennifer," Leo repeated, as if it were the most uniquely beautiful name he'd ever heard.

Elise poked her head through the rush-hour crowd and narrowed her blue eyes at Jenny. "Hey, I'm sorry I pushed you. Are you okay?"

Leo smiled his adorable chip-toothed smile at her as if to say that any friend of Jenny's was a friend of his. Jenny's first instinct was to snarl at Elise to buzz off so she and Leo could get acquainted in peace. But she didn't want Leo to think she was a total bitch. The man seated next to her stood up and Jenny patted the seat. "Sit down."

Elise let go of the handrail and plunked herself down in the seat. "Hey," she said, looking up at Leo. She clacked her knee against Jenny's leg when she recognized him. "*Hey.*"

"Elise, this is Leo. Leo, this is Elise," Jenny introduced them sweetly. The bus halted abruptly and Leo reached for her shoulder to steady himself. *Oh, God. He touched me! He touched me!*

Jenny could feel Elise studying them as she tried to figure out what was going on.

"Do you go to Constance Billard, too?" Leo asked Elise.

Elise nodded, looking totally confused. All of a sudden, Jenny felt bad for her. She put her arm around her friend and smiled up at Leo. "We're best friends."

Elise giggled and let her head fall on Jenny's shoulder. "I guess you found your hat," she whispered quietly.

"Yup," Jenny giggled back, relieved that Elise was cool enough not to ask too many questions. When they were alone, she would explain everything, just like best friends were supposed to. She gazed up at Leo's perfectly structured, perfectly paintable face, swooning as he flashed his shy, chipped-tooth smile again. "I knew your name couldn't be Lance."

v turns down chance to film decomposing fish bodies!

"Glad you could make it," Ken Mogul said on Wednesday afternoon when Vanessa joined him at a booth in Chippies, the new Williamsburg coffee shop down the street from where she lived. He pushed a steaming mug of cappuccino toward her. "I ordered for both of us. Hope that's cool by you."

Vanessa sat down with her black down parka on and clasped the mug with both hands, pursing her lips as she blew on the hot, milky froth. "Thanks for hooking me up with that whole fashion show gig," she said. "It was such a gas." She winced, hating the way she sounded when she talked to Ken Mogul. Like some brainless poser fool.

Ken pushed his tortoise-shell Persol sunglasses up on top of his jauntily cut red hair and leaned across the table, ready to get down to business. "I'd like you to join me at Cannes this spring. I'll introduce you to some other brilliant independent filmmakers. We can trade energy, brainstorm together. Then I want you to hold off on college for a year or two to make some films with me. It's going to be magical, I can feel it."

Enya was playing over the sound system. Vanessa unzipped her coat and then zipped it up again. She hated Enya.

"I've started working on a new project down in South

America," Ken Mogul continued. "It opens with sea gulls feeding their young the flesh from decomposing fish bodies and then moves to gorillas in the rainforest abandoning their young. Then I'm going to cut to the streets of Rio, where kids are prostituting themselves for drugs. I haven't begun filming yet, but I was thinking you could get in there and meet some of the kids, *befriend* them, get their *stories*. You don't happen to know Portuguese, do you?"

Vanessa shook her head. Who was he kidding?

"Spanish?"

She shook her head again.

"It doesn't matter. We'll get a translator, or find some kids who speak English. All your expenses will be paid for by Duke Productions. You remember Duke from the Better Than Naked party?"

Vanessa nodded with an amused smile. How could she forget Duke, the dumbest guy on the planet?

"You'd have your own car, your own apartment, free equipment, and whatever else you need," Ken added. "Are you with me?"

Vanessa noticed for the first time that Ken Mogul had very little definition in the chin area. In fact, he was practically chinless. "I've always wanted to go to Cannes," she replied, thoughtfully slurping her cappuccino. "And your new project sounds really . . . awesome. But I got accepted early to NYU. I've wanted to go there since I was eleven years old. There's no way I'm deferring."

"But what about my film? Child prostitution! Animals abandoning their young! This is groundbreaking stuff!" Ken Mogul spluttered, spitting all over the counter. Vanessa thought that if he'd had more of a chin, the spit might not have gone so far.

Over Ken's shoulder Vanessa noticed a light blue flyer pinned to a bulletin board.

Rivington Rover Poetry Club Open Mike
featuring readings by
Daniel Humphrey and Mystery Craze
Thursday, 8 P.M.

No wonder Dan had been blowing her off all week. He was busy being famous.

"Vanessa? Are you still with me?" Ken demanded. "First lesson you learn in this business is the clock never stops ticking."

Vanessa smiled her half-amused, half-pissed-off Mona Lisa smile. As flattered as she was that Ken had asked her to work with him, she had no intention of becoming a mini-Mogul. She wanted to develop her *own* voice and her *own* career, not put all her energy into someone else's work, however brilliant. She shook her closely shaved dark head. "I'm sorry."

Ken Mogul's barely there chin disappeared altogether as he lost his cool completely. "I've never offered to partner with anyone," he said grimly. "This is the opportunity of a lifetime. I'm giving you the chance to make a feature film before you turn twenty. It's unheard of!"

That old guy at the Culture of Humanity show had advised her not to take her talent too seriously. Ken obviously took his way, *way* too seriously. She stood up and yanked the light blue flyer off the bulletin board behind Ken's head. She and Dan were supposed to be working on a film *together*, but if she could slip into the club and film him reading without him even knowing she was there, that would be even better. Dan was always better when he didn't know she was watching.

"Thank you," she told Ken. "I'm honored, I really am.

But I'm working on something new, of my own. I think I'd like to finish it."

Ken Mogul pushed his sunglasses down on his nose and glared out the window. "It's your loss."

"Thanks for the coffee," Vanessa said, even though he was no longer looking at her. She folded up the blue flyer and tucked it into her pocket. "Good luck at Cannes."

Ken Mogul zipped up his fur-trimmed Prada parka and pulled the hood up over his head as if to block her out completely. "'Bye."

Vanessa headed home to sort through her camera gear and figure out what she needed to bring to the reading at the Rivington Rover Poetry Club tomorrow night. When Dan was finished reading she'd pop up out of the crowd and surprise him with an enormous mug of Irish coffee, his favorite drink. Then they'd trade stories about all the feebleminded famous people they'd met in the past week. And then she'd bring him home and remind him of what he'd been missing. She'd show him how to lose his virginity again the way he'd written in that crazy poem.

As if he needed showing.

s reinvents the tear

"Want to take Mook out for a walk with me?" Aaron asked Blair through her closed bedroom door. It was Wednesday afternoon and she'd been holed up in her room since Monday, only opening the door to receive the brie-and-tomato baguettes and mugs of hot chocolate Myrtle brought her at ten and five o'clock. She'd even conned the family doctor into writing her a note excusing her from school for the week. She wasn't sick exactly, the doctor assured her mother. Schools like Constance just worked their girls too hard, especially the seniors, and then there was all that additional pressure to get into one of the best colleges. Blair simply needed a few days of rest and she'd be herself again.

Well, not exactly. Blair was using her few days of rest to reinvent herself all over again. Like Madonna.

Aaron pushed open the door and poked his head inside her room. The air was pungent with the chemical odor of cigarette smoke mixed with minty mouthwash. Blair's head was wrapped in a black-and-pink Pucci scarf, and she was lounging on the bed with her bare ankles crossed, wearing a white terrycloth robe and smoking a Merit Ultra Light through a long black cigarette holder. The look was very Greta-Garbo-in-hiding, which was exactly the effect she was going for.

Across the room, *The Great Gatsby* starring Robert Redford and Mia Farrow played silently on TV. Blair puffed on her cigarette, staring dramatically into the near distance. She couldn't bear to look at Aaron because he was wearing his Harvard sweatshirt again, as if he'd specifically dressed to piss her off. She'd already ripped her Yale pendant off the canopy over her bed and thrown it out her bedroom window along with her father's old Yale sweatshirt. "If you don't mind, I'd like you to please get the fuck out of my room."

"I was just leaving," Aaron replied. "Hey, have you talked to Serena lately?"

Blair shook her head. "Why?"

"No reason," Aaron shrugged uncomfortably. He'd been hanging out with his buddies in Scarsdale since Friday night and hadn't seen or talked to Serena since the Les Best show. He pulled a tin of herbal cigarettes out of his back pocket and tossed them onto Blair's bed. "Try those," he advised. "They're 100 percent natural and they smell way better than that mass-produced shit."

Blair kicked the tin onto the floor. "Have a nice walk."

Aaron pulled her bedroom door closed behind him and headed outside with Mookie. He entered the park at Seventy-second Street, taking the path that led to a little wooden foot-bridge over a stream that fed into the lake. Every now and then Mookie stopped to dig furiously in the snow with his brown-and-white paws, as if he were looking for a doggie toy he'd dropped there last summer. Then eventually he'd give up and trot on again.

A petite blond in dark sunglasses and a blue Yankees cap jogged by wearing an I LOVE AARON T-shirt over her red velour tracksuit; the same I LOVE AARON T-shirt that Serena had worn at the Les Best show. Aaron was pretty sure the blond was the actress Renee Zwingdinger, or whatever her name was, but he couldn't be sure. It was pretty funny to think that famous actresses and models might be wearing shirts with his name on them when he was just some dude who went out with a beautiful girl who he guessed he wasn't really going out with anymore.

When the wooden footbridge came into view, Aaron noticed that it was filled with people and equipment, a crew of some sort. As he came closer he saw that in the icy water opposite the footbridge a cameraman was standing up in a small inflatable raft, adjusting his tripod.

Aaron let Mookie hunt for squirrels under a tree as he watched the proceedings. The huddle of people on the bridge parted to reveal a girl dressed in a skimpy sunflower yellow sundress and blue sandals, her golden hair blowing in the icy wind. It was Serena, of course. She was unmistakable.

All of a sudden Mookie hurtled across the snow in Serena's direction, howling with delight and wagging his stubby little boxer tail.

"Mookie, no!" Aaron shouted. Everyone on the bridge, including Serena, turned to look.

"Mookie!" Serena squealed, crouching down to kiss the dog on his wet nose as he wriggled excitedly between her legs. "How's it going, handsome?"

Aaron ambled over to the footbridge, his hands shoved deep into his green army pants pockets. "Sorry," he mumbled to the crew of makeup artists and stylists.

"That's okay," Serena said, standing up. She broke away from her entourage and kissed Aaron lightly on the cheek. Her yellow dress was stenciled with iridescent blue birds and her lip gloss smelled like watermelon. "We're just shooting a perfume ad. You can watch if you want to."

Aaron kept his hands in his pockets. There were a million things she could have said to make him feel guilty for hiding out in Scarsdale and never calling her, but Serena was too cool for that. She was truly magnificent, which was part of the reason he had to let her go. It was too much effort to match someone who shone as brightly as she did.

"Don't let me keep you," Aaron said. He opened his tin of herbal cigarettes and offered her one. She took it and held it between her coral-glossed lips as he lit it for her. "Oh, and thanks for the roses."

Serena exhaled, blowing sweet smoke into the chilly air. "We never got our tattoos."

Aaron smiled tenderly. "That's probably a good thing."

A perfect tear began to form in the corner of Serena's right eye and trembled on the edge of her lower lid.

"Let's get this done!" the photographer shouted from his inflatable boat.

Serena turned to wave at him, her yellow dress fanning out around her knees and her blond hair flying. In that instant, the tear dropped onto her lovely cheek, a perfect illustration of every human emotion Les Best wanted to encapsulate in his new perfume ad. They'd have to airbrush out the cigarette in Serena's hand and the goosebumps dotting her arms and legs, but you'd be surprised how easy that is to do.

rehab is the new spa

After watching *The Great Gatsby* twice in a row, Blair clicked off the TV and picked up her phone. She was eager to talk to someone; to let the world know she was still alive despite everything. The thing was, she absolutely *dreaded* speaking to every single person she knew, including her gay, France-living dad, whom she had always counted on to cheer her up. If only there were someone else, someone new and different who—

Actually, there was *one* person she could bear to speak to. And why the fuck shouldn't she call him when he had called her completely out of the blue last week while she was getting her hair cut?

She speed-dialed Nate's cell phone number, and, to her surprise, he answered it.

"Natie?" Blair crooned into the phone. "I heard all about what happened. How *are* you? Are you okay?"

"Yeah, actually I'm really good," Nate responded, sounding suspiciously unstoned. "My dad's still pretty pissed off about what happened, and I don't know how it's going to affect my chances at Brown, but I'm still good."

Blair pointed her bare toes into the air and frowned at the day-old cotton-candy-pink polish that she'd painted on herself out of complete boredom. "You poor baby," she sighed sympathetically. "Rehab must totally suck."

"Um, actually—and I know this sounds weird—I'm starting to kind of *like* it," Nate admitted. "I wish it wasn't such a haul to get up there, but it's a really cool, modern place, and it's kind of, I don't know . . . *relaxing* to do something totally unrelated to school."

"Really?" Blair fluffed up the pillows behind her and sat up in bed. Rehab was *relaxing*? Maybe it was exactly what she needed—a respite from the travails of her quotidian existence. She could picture herself wrapped in a downy white spa robe, her face lathered in green clay masque, her feet and hands stuck with acupuncture needles, sipping detoxifying herbal tea as she lounged on a daybed chatting to an attentive counselor in a white linen tunic.

"If you could be any sort of animal, what would you be?" the counselor would ask her. Nothing too challenging.

Rehab. Why hadn't she thought of it before? Sure, there might be a little therapy involved, but she'd never had a problem talking about herself. And best of all, *Nate would be there*—the two of them alone together, away from the city and all its messy baggage. She'd always dreamed of spending a weekend with Nate at a romantic bed-and-breakfast on the Cape or in the Hamptons. A rehab clinic in Greenwich, Connecticut, would be almost as good. Sure, she'd thought she'd wanted to erase Nate's arrogant, cheating presence from her life entirely, but Nate sounded like he was turning over a new leaf, which was exactly what she was trying to do!

"So how do you get into rehab anyway? Can you just sign up, or do you have to be sent there by somebody?" Blair asked. She glanced at herself in the mirror on the back of her closet door. With her hacked-off hair and pasty face, she looked enough like a heroin addict that they were sure to admit her.

"I think you can sign yourself in, but who'd be crazy enough to do that?" Nate asked.

Blair smiled. *She would.* "So do you want to get together tomorrow night or something?" she asked. "I know I act like a bitch sometimes, Nate, but I always wind up missing you."

"Sorry. I have to be at Breakaway for group," Nate responded. He hadn't seen Georgie since the night of the snowstorm and Jackie had promised Georgie would be returning to group tomorrow. "I take the train, so I don't get home until pretty late."

"All right. But let's get together sometime soon, okay?" Blair said. "You know you love me," she added in a seductive whisper and hung up.

Hopping off her bed with newfound energy, she removed the Pucci scarf from her head and messed up what little hair she had left with a dime-sized squirt of Bed Head texturizing hair gel. Then she opened her bedroom door for the first time all week. "Mom!" she shouted down the hall. "Come quick. I need your help with something!"

What better way for the leading lady to make a comeback than to emerge from rehab, refreshed and rejuvenated, with her handsome leading man at her side?

gossipgirl.net

topics ◄ *previous* *next* ▶ *post a question* reply

hey people!

Serena's Tears

The Les Best people didn't waste any time getting their new perfume ad out and by now you've all seen it. Magnifique, non? The perfume's not available until April unless, like me, you have access to things no one else does. It's a heady jasmine scent with subtle undertones of sandalwood and patchouli. I'm wearing it right now and I have to admit it's just as divine as the ad. But when a certain blond is involved, we wouldn't expect any less would we?

Teen heiress donates portion of inheritance to rehab

It seems **N**'s poor little rich girl has been bitten by the generosity bug. To show her gratitude to those who have helped her in the last few weeks she's funding the construction of state-of-the-art stables on Breakaway's rambling Connecticut property. The stables will house horses, pigs, goats, dogs, cats, and chickens, which will be used for therapeutic purposes, of course. Apparently milking goats can work wonders on the drug-addled minds of coke fiends. Let's just hope our beloved heiress keeps her hands off the stables' medicine cabinet!

Your e-mail

Hi GG,
I'm an outpatient at Breakaway and I was there today when this girl with messy short hair and fur boots came in and tossed her platinum credit card at the nurse at reception. She wanted to book a private room for two weeks, preferably with a view of the fountain.

Hello? They told her she couldn't stay there unless she was harmful to herself or others, but that she was welcome to come to teen group if she wanted.
—sun

A:
Hello sun,
I'm surprised she didn't try booking a series of facials! If you're in teen group I'd steer clear of her. It sounds like she's on a mission.
—GG

Sightings

J and her two new pals at **Bowlmor Lanes**. They look so cute together, but I've been there, and threesomes never work. **S** home sick from school on Friday with bronchitis. That will teach her to wear sundresses in February! **B** shopping for her rehab outfit in a vintage store on **Mulberry Street**. If she's going to get the part of the desperate junkie, she has to look authentic. **D** practicing for the **Rivington Rover Poetry Club** open mike on the subway, whispering to himself over the clackety-clack of the train.

It's time to get out and do something cultural for once. See you at the open mike tonight!

You know you love me.

gossip girl

for the sake of her art

"I'm glad you're here," Dan told Mystery as she ran her chewed-on, yellow-nailed fingers through his fashionably tousled hair. By total coincidence he and Mystery had arrived at the Rivington Rover Poetry club at the same time, and for the last fifteen minutes they'd been smoking unfiltered Camels and groping each other in a stall in the graffiti-ridden ladies' room, trying to get psyched up for their reading. "I'm kind of nervous."

"Don't be," Mystery loosened his narrow black tie and clasped his hand. "Come on. Let's see what we've got."

They emerged from the ladies' room hand in hand, Mystery in a transparent canary yellow silk sheath through which her black cotton underwear was completely visible, and Dan in his new black suit: the Bonnie and Clyde of poetry.

The small, dark basement club was already crowded with people sipping coffee and lounging on the tattered old sofas haphazardly dotting the room. A random disco ball spun from the black ceiling and over the sound system Morrissey whined a depressing song from his latest album.

The lights blinked on and off twice and a tiny Japanese girl wearing a black leotard and pink ballet tights took the stage. "Welcome all to open mike at Rivington Rover. It is so special to have you here," she whispered into the microphone. "Tonight two of New York's most special poets will recite for us simultaneously. I'm honored to give the stage to Mystery Craze and Daniel Humphrey!"

The dark, crowded room erupted in applause.

"I heard they stayed up all night on E and wrote a book together," somebody whispered.

"I heard they were husband and wife."

"I heard they're fraternal twins, separated at birth," remarked someone else.

Vanessa slipped into the back of the club unnoticed. "What kind of name is Mystery Craze?" she wondered as she put her camera to her eye and zoomed in on the stage.

Dan's entire body was covered in a cold, freaked-out sweat. Everything was happening so fast. He hadn't even had a chance to contemplate how he'd gone from writing strange, morose poetry in notebooks no one ever read to performing onstage with an almost-famous girl in a cool club, wearing a fancy designer suit. But there was no time to doubt himself. He'd acted in plays, performed in Vanessa's movies. He was the new Rilke. He peeled off his jacket, and rolled up his sleeves. He could do this.

Mystery was already waiting for him onstage, her bony fingers clenching the microphone in white-knuckled anticipation. Dan could see now that there were two mikes, one for him and one for her.

"What's your favorite noun?" Mystery asked the audience in her low, husky voice.

"Pie!" an obviously shitfaced ponytailed guy in the front row shouted back.

"You're the antithesis of pie," Mystery hissed at Dan as he took the stage. "I want to eat you alive."

Dan cleared his throat and reached for the microphone

stand to steady himself. "What's your favorite verb?" he asked in response, surprised by how sure of himself he sounded.

"Sex," Mystery answered coolly. She dropped to her hands and knees, slithering toward him with the microphone between her teeth. "Sex," she repeated, crawling between his legs and clawing her way up his body until their faces were only a centimeter apart. The yellow dress made her teeth look even yellower.

The camera wobbled in Vanessa's hands. So *this* was why she hadn't heard a peep out of Dan lately, not even to work on *Making Poetry*. Dan had been making poetry with Mystery Craze. And as much as it hurt to watch the boy she'd been in love with for almost three years fall under the spell of a girl whose real name was probably something totally boring and unpoetic like Jane James, Vanessa couldn't bring herself to stop filming. Something was happening to Dan that she had to get on film. He seemed to be discovering himself, right before her eyes.

"Feed me," Dan growled into the mike as Mystery writhed beneath him. "Bare your naked body on my plate."

The crowded whooped and shrieked in delight. Dan couldn't believe what a total blast he was having. He was a rock'n'roll poet, a sex god! Forget Rilke, he was Jim Morrison! He dragged Mystery off the floor and dove at her mouth in a hard and hungry rock-god kiss.

Vanessa kept filming, hot tears streaming down her pale cheeks. She couldn't stop, and she wasn't doing it to torture herself. She was doing it for the sake of her art.

Onstage, Dan unbuttoned his shirt and Mystery licked his chest.

"Oh, Daddy," she whispered huskily.

Oh, *brother*.

diva makes her entrance

"Welcome, everyone," Jackie Davis greeted Breakaway's Friday afternoon teen therapy group. "I'm so pleased to welcome back our old friend Georgina Spark." She tapped her pencil against her clipboard. "We're also expecting a new friend today. But while we're waiting for her I'd like to recognize two members of the group for their courage and for demonstrating what I like to call *life-building* for the rest of us." She beamed an encouraging smile at Nate. "Nate, would you like to tell us about what happened last Friday now that Georgie is back?"

Nate tipped his chair back and then righted it again. Across the circle from him Georgie was sitting with her legs crossed, wearing orange satin short shorts and orange leather sandals, which was kind of a strange choice for the middle of February, but it wasn't like she went outside very much these days. Her luxurious dark hair clung to her Snow White face as she looked up at him with a coy smile on her dark red lips.

Nate rubbed his hands against his olive green Ralph Lauren cords. God, he wished he could kiss her. The other members of the group were waiting eagerly. They knew some serious shit had gone down but they still hadn't heard the whole story.

"Go on, Nate," Jackie prompted.

"Friday night I was over at Georgie's house and we were having a good time, um, getting to know each other," he began to explain. "Then I figured out that Georgie was kind of having her own separate little party in the medicine cabinet. When she conked out I got kind of worried. So I called Jackie."

"It was a cry for help," Georgie intoned with mock enthusiasm.

Nate chuckled to himself. She was still a mess, but so fucking irresistible. And he was glad he had to go to rehab for six whole months, because he actually wanted to help her the way she had helped him.

"We got her to the clinic just in time. She's going to live here for a while, and she's been doing wonderfully so far, haven't you Georgie?" Jackie gushed.

Georgie nodded and hugged herself, a placid smile plastered to her face. "The meatloaf at dinner last night was not to be believed."

"Let's put our hands together and give them both props for their courage!" Jackie cried. Every member of the group stood up and applauded, including Georgie and Nate.

"Hey," Georgie mouthed to Nate and licked her bloodred lips.

"Hey," Nate mouthed back.

"Right this way, miss."

Blair smoothed down her freshly plucked eyebrows and rubbed her pink-glossed lips together as she followed one of Breakaway's linen-clad staff members to the room where the teen group therapy session was already under way. She was wearing her new vintage black, red, and purple Diane von Furstenberg wrap dress paired with her favorite pair of pointy black suede knee-high boots, and she was positively brimming with excitement at the idea of spilling her guts in front of a rapt audience that would include Nate.

"Welcome, Blair Waldorf," a dowdy woman wearing ugly brown lipstick greeted her when the staff member opened the door. She walked over and ushered Blair into the room. "I'm Jackie Davis, the teen group facilitator. Please come in and have a seat."

Blair surveyed the group. There was Natie, her Nate, looking scrumptious as ever in his olive green cords which set off his wonderful green eyes. To her dismay, the only empty chair was next to this Jackie person who Blair could already tell was a total drip.

"You can all sit down again," Jackie instructed, taking her seat. "Now, what we like to do when a new member joins the group is go around the circle saying who we are and naming the thing or the circumstance that brought us here. Be as specific and concise as possible. Remember, naming your weakness is the first step toward taking control of it. Don't worry, Blair," Jackie put a reassuring hand on Blair's arm, "I won't make you go first. Billy, would you like to begin?"

A stocky, muscular boy in a white Dartmouth sweatshirt rubbed his hands together nervously. "I'm Billy White. I'm addicted to lifting weights and drinking muscle-building drinks," he announced. "I'm an exercise bulimic."

Nate was next. He couldn't believe Blair had actually turned up at Breakaway, but he'd known her long enough not to put anything past her. "I'm Nate and I used to smoke marijuana every day, but I have to say, lately I haven't really wanted to." It was sort of strange to admit this in front of Blair, the girl from back in the days when he'd been permanently stoned.

Blair's eyebrows shot up in pleased surprise. Was Nate really reforming? Was he doing it for *her*?

"I'm Hannah Koto," said the girl sitting next to Nate. "I've taken E every day since my dog died last summer." She glanced at Jackie. "Sorry. *Ecstasy*," she clarified.

"I'm Campbell and I'm a budding alcoholic," said a blond boy who looked no older than ten. "I cleaned out my parents' wine cellars in Darien and Cape Cod."

"I'm Georgie and I'll do anything," said a strikingly beautiful girl with long, silky brown hair, enormous brown eyes, and dark red lips. She was wearing orange satin Miu Miu short shorts and beautiful tangerine leather Jimmy Choo sandals, Blair noted enviously. "Lately I like pills and I used to be scared that one day I'd fall asleep and never wake up again. But now that I know I have a knight in shining armor . . ." She batted her thick brown eyelashes in Nate's direction. Blair's hackles rose.

"Thank you, Georgie," Jackie interrupted before Georgie could say anything that might jeopardize her control over the group. "Next?"

"I'm Jodia and I'm an alcoholic, too," said the chubby girl sitting next to Blair. "I even drank perfume once."

"Me too," Blair cut in, eager to top Georgie's performance. She uncrossed and recrossed her legs, giving the room a glimpse of her sexy black fishnets through the slit in her dress. "I'm Blair and . . ." She hesitated. Where to begin? She took a deep, dramatic breath.

"My parents got divorced last year. It turns out my father was gay and he was fooling around with my mom's personal assistant, who was only twenty-one. They're still together, and now they live in a château in a vineyard in France. My mother just married this gross fat freak real estate developer and now they're having a baby, even though she's, like, a hundred years old. It's a girl, they just found out. I was supposed to apply early to Yale, but my interview sucked. So this old friend of my father's said he'd give me an alumni interview. He was really attractive and I'd never been with an older guy before so I kind of hooked up with him," she glanced apologetically at Nate. He'd forgive her for philandering, just as she'd forgive him for straying from her.

Jackie listened with her mouth agape. She was used to the kids in teen group giving a little more detail than was necessary, but she'd never run across anyone who seemed to enjoy talking about herself so much.

"I think part of the reason I cut all my hair off was I was trying to make myself ugly, even though I didn't realize it at the time. I thought short hair might look cool on me. But I think I was maybe, you know, bringing all the ugliness inside to the surface? And this past week I stayed home from school. I wasn't really sick, I just couldn't—"

"I'm sorry to interrupt, but if you could simply name your problem—," Jackie broke in when she realized Blair wasn't even close to being finished.

Blair frowned and twisted her little ruby ring around and around on her finger. It sounded like she had to have a *specific* problem or they'd kick her out. "Sometimes when I'm upset—which, considering what my life is like now, is all the time—I eat too much, or I eat something that I shouldn't, and then I make myself sick." *There*, that sounded convincing.

Jackie nodded. "Can you name your problem, Blair? There's a name for that, you know."

Blair glared at her. "Stress-induced regurgitation?" she answered tightly. She knew Jackie wanted her to say *bulimia*, but it was such a gross word, she refused to say it, especially in front of Nate. Bulimia was for losers.

The rest of the room tittered. Jackie was eager to get the

group back on track after Blair's soliloquy. "Well, I suppose that's one way of putting it," she noted, marking something on her clipboard.

She looked up and smoothed back her wiry brown hair. "Now it's my turn. I'm Jackie Davis and my job is to help you *break away!*" She punched her fist into the air and let out a little whoop like she was at a basketball game and her team had just scored. She waited for the members of the group to punch the air with their fists and whoop along with her, but they just stared at her blankly. "All right. Good. Now I want you all to pair up. We're going to do a little exercise I like to call 'Go to hell, demon!' One of you is going to be the thing you just named, the thing you're trying to break away from. I want the other person to stand in your face and tell that demon where to go. Tell it anything you want, but do it with *feeling*. Make it *real*. Okay, go ahead, pair up. There's only seven of us, so someone will have to pair with me."

Hannah raised her hand. "Wait. Are we talking to *their* demon or our own demon?"

"*Your* demon," Jackie clarified. "This is going to help you exorcise it!"

Blair waited for Nate to walk over to her, but before he even had a chance the pale bitch in the totally inappropriate orange satin short shorts minced up to him and took his hand. "Be my partner?" Blair heard her whine. Everyone else had already paired up, so Blair was stuck with Jackie.

"All right, Blair!" Jackie screeched at her. She was wearing clumpy brown mascara and her eyes were toad brown. "Let's tell that demon where to go!"

Suddenly Blair wondered if rehab was really the right place for her. "I have to go to the bathroom," she announced. Hopefully the exercise would be over when she got back, and she might be able to snag a seat next to Nate before they all sat down again.

Jackie eyed her suspiciously. "Okay, but make it quick. And let me remind you that all the restrooms are monitored."

Blair rolled her eyes as she pushed open the door and walked across the hall to the ladies' room. She washed her hands and reapplied her lip gloss, pulling open her dress and flashing the mirrors with her bare chest, just to give whoever was watching a cheap thrill. Then she walked back across the hall and peeked in the door again, checking to see if they'd finished the exercise.

Nate and that Miu Miu short shorts–clad slut Georgie were standing near the door. She had her hands on Nate's shoulders and their faces were only inches apart.

"I've been thinking of a way to thank you for the roses," Blair thought she heard Short Shorts whisper. "I want to give you a pony ride."

She wasn't talking to her demon, Blair realized. She was talking to *Nate*.

Blair waited for Nate to express his horror and disgust at what Short Shorts was saying, but all he did was grin at her with his tongue lolling, like he couldn't wait to hear more.

"I'm going to cover you with—" Blair didn't wait to hear the rest of Georgie's sentence. It was pretty obvious why Nate liked rehab so much and why he was so into reforming all of a sudden. She backed out the door and into the hall, pulling her cell phone out of her purse to call her mom. A car was supposed to come and get her in two hours to drive her back to the city, but no way was she waiting that long. Rehab was nothing like a spa; it was just another classroom full of pathetic losers who needed to get a life.

"You can't use that in here, miss!" an aide shouted at her in the hallway. Blair glared at her and marched down the hall and into the lobby. One of the receptionists was reading a newspaper with a full-page color ad for Serena's Tears on the back.

Suddenly something occurred to Blair. She'd never really thought about it before but Serena van der Woodsen— her supposed best friend—was the absolute queen of comebacks. This past fall Serena had been kicked out of boarding school and had come home to the city, her reputation so smeared only the most desperate wanna-bes would talk to her. But in a series of show-stealing cameos Serena had won everyone back, Blair included, and now she was the star of a fucking international perfume ad campaign. If anyone could help Blair shimmy her way back to the top and make everyone fall in love with her again, Serena could.

Blair pushed open the glass doors of the rehab clinic and stood at the top of the marble steps, gasping in the cold. Quickly, she punched Serena's number into her cell phone.

"Blair?" Serena shouted, her phone cutting in and out. "I thought you were mad at me." She coughed loudly. "God, am I sick."

"Where are you?" Blair demanded in response. "Are you in a cab?"

"Right," Serena answered. "I'm going to a movie premiere with some people I met at the perfume shoot. Want to come?"

"I can't," Blair answered. "Serena, I need you to come get me. Tell the cab to take I-95 up to Greenwich. Exit 3. There's this place called Breakaway on Lake Avenue. Get him to stop and ask someone if he can't find it. Okay?"

"Greenwich? But that's going to cost like a hundred bucks!" Serena argued. "What's going on, Blair? Why are you in Greenwich? This doesn't have anything to do with that old guy I saw you with the other night, does it?"

"I'll pay you back," Blair interrupted impatiently. "I'll tell you all about it when you get here. Will you do it, S?" she asked, using the endearment she hadn't used since they were little.

Serena hesitated, but Blair could tell she was intrigued by the idea of an adventure with her old friend. The phone crackled as she heard Serena give the driver directions.

"I have to hang up because my phone is running out of juice," Serena yelled. "I'll be there soon, Blair, okay? Oh, and by the way, Aaron and I broke up."

Blair sucked cold air in through her nostrils, her freshly glossed lips turning up in a smug smile as she absorbed the information. "We'll talk about it when you get here." Clicking off, she sat down on the cold, hard steps and buttoned up her sky blue cashmere toggle coat, pulling the hood up over her head before firing up a Merit Ultra Light. If anyone had passed by on the road, they'd have seen a mysterious girl in a blue hooded coat, looking defiantly sure of herself, even though the plot had changed and the script had to be entirely rewritten.

what we talk about when we're not talking about love

"Everyone get their coats," Serena told the ninth graders in peer group on Monday. "We're taking you out for hot chocolate at Jackson Hole."

"Don't worry, we have permission," Blair added, checking herself out in the cafeteria mirror. She'd gone back to the salon to have her hair touched up and now she looked like Edie Sedgwick from the Andy Warhol Factory days. It was totally far out.

"Wow," Jenny breathed, staring at her. "You look great." Jenny was so happy since meeting Leo, she was practically bursting with love for everyone she encountered.

Blair turned around, remembering something. "Have you been checking your e-mail?" she demanded.

Jenny's eyes lit up. "Oh, yes. Yes, I have!"

Blair thought about taking credit for Jenny's obvious state of complete ecstasy, but it was actually more fun to watch Jenny glow in complete oblivion. Maybe it wouldn't be so horrible being a big sister after all. She noticed Elise Wells was wearing a tight black cropped sweater instead of one of her trademark prissy pink cardigans. Good. Maybe her mom had finally murdered her father for being such an asshole.

"How are things with your dad, Elise?" Serena asked, practically reading Blair's mind.

To Blair's surprise, Elise smiled happily. "Fine. He and Mom went away together this weekend." She laughed and nudged Jenny in the arm. "But never mind me. I think Jenny has something to say."

Jenny knew her face was beet red, but she didn't care. "I'm in love," she declared.

Serena and Blair exchanged disparaging looks. The last thing they wanted to talk about was *love*. "Come on, get your coats," Serena urged. "We'll meet you outside."

The atmosphere in Jackson Hole on Madison Avenue was thick with the smell of hamburger grease and the tittering sound of gossip. As peer group A walked in and sat down at a table near the large glass windows, Kati Farkas and Isabel Coates huddled together in the back corner, discussing the latest developments with anyone who would listen.

"Did you hear about Nate Archibald and that girl from Connecticut?" Kati asked. She'd had her hair cut short over the weekend and it made her Germanic nose look twice its size. "They got busted for having sex in the broom closet at rehab and now he has to go to private therapy in the city instead."

"Wait, I thought it was *Blair* and Nate in the broom closet," Isabel sniffed. She was wearing a sample of Serena's Tears that she'd gotten from her mom's publicist friend who worked at *Vogue*. It made her nose run.

"No, stupid. Blair is seeing that old guy, remember? She's not having his baby anymore, though. She had a miscarriage. That's why she missed so much school."

"I heard that Blair and Serena both sent in applications to the University of California school system today," said Laura Salmon. "They have rolling admission, so you find out which

UC school can take you, like, a few weeks after you apply." She raised her thin strawberry blond eyebrows. "Hey, maybe we should all do that!"

Not that any of them would *really* have considered going to a UC school.

"So what was it like, being in that perfume ad?" Mary Goldberg asked Serena while the girls in peer group A were waiting for their hot chocolates. Cassie Inwirth and Vicky Reinerson pricked their ears up on either side of her. The three girls had gotten matching short haircuts over the week-end, but since none of them had gone to see Gianni at Garren, their cuts were only pale imitations of Blair's old one, and *nothing* compared to her new one.

"Cold," Serena answered. She blew her nose on a paper napkin and then pulled her long, golden blond hair up on top of her head, twisted it into a bun, and stuck a pencil through it to hold it up.

Of course now they all wished they hadn't cut their hair.

"I'd really rather not talk about it," she added mysteriously.

Blair leaned across the table. "She and Aaron broke up during the shoot," she told the ninth graders in a confidential whisper. She sat up straight again. "End of subject."

The waiter brought their hot chocolates, giant steaming mugs, loaded with Reddi-wip.

"Can we talk about love now?" Jenny asked tremulously. She glanced around the crowded room. If she was lucky, Leo might even show up so she could show him off.

"No!" Serena and Blair cried in unison. They'd specifically brought the group to Jackson Hole so they wouldn't have to talk about boys, food, parents, school, *anything*. All they wanted was to sip their hot chocolates and enjoy each other's company.

Suddenly a hush fell over the restaurant as Chuck Bass waltzed in wearing a fox fur hat and a baby blue pea coat, his monogrammed pinky ring flashing as he passed out pink flyers to everyone inside.

"Be there or be square!" he shouted, drifting out the door in a cloud of Serena's Tears just as suddenly as he had come in.

The flyer was an invitation to a party on Monday night, and within seconds the entire restaurant was positively humming.

"Are you going?"

"Wait. Do you think it's really Chuck's *coming out* party?

"No. It's his birthday. Can't you read?"

"But we went to nursery school together. His birthday is in *September*. It's not even his party. It's some girl's. He's just handing out the flyers."

"I still think he's bi. I saw him with a girl from L'École Française on Saturday, and they were practically *doing it*."

"Who was that guy anyway?" Cassie Inwirth whined.

"You know that site www.gossipgirl.net? Well, I think that's him!" Mary Goldberg announced.

"You think Gossip Girl is a he?" Vicky Reinerson countered.

"No way!" Serena and Blair cried.

You never know.

hey people!

Not that I'm greedy or anything

By now you've all seen the flyer inviting everyone to my party Monday night. And if you haven't, where have you been—hiding under a rock? Please don't bother to turn up unless you bring one of the following:

A caramel toy poodle puppy

As many bottles of Serena's Tears as you can scrape up. I know there's a waiting list, but I'm addicted!

First-class tickets to Cannes this May

Diamonds

A fantastic sense of humor

Every gorgeous boy in your address book

Sightings

N and his über-rich, pale new girlfriend on a carriage ride in **Central Park**. Guess she got a day pass from rehab for good behavior. **S** and **B** in the **Les Best** boutique getting fitted for his entire fall line. **V** delivering a manila envelope to the drama department at **Riverside Prep**. You don't think she actually turned in that film to **D**'s drama teacher do you? Now that's dedication! **D** and that crazy poetess shouting non-sequiturs out the window of her **Chinatown** studio. Little **J** and her new beau checking out tattoos in **Stink**, an East Village tattoo parlor. Let's pray they were only browsing.

As for those burning questions . . .

Will **N** and his misbehaving heiress remain a bona fide item?

Will **B** *ever* get over **N**? Will she grow out her hair? And—thank God the answer is just around the corner—will she get into Yale??

Will **S** and **B** remain friends . . . at least until graduation?

Will **S** become a vapid, redundant, celery-eating supermodel? Will she ever stay with one guy for more than five minutes?

Will **J** and her new boy live happily ever after? Will her new best friend try to break them up?

Will **V** ever even *look* at **D** again?

Will **D** keep hanging out with that yellow-toothed poetess? Will *his* teeth turn yellow in the process? Will he actually write a memoir?

Will the rest of us get into college? More importantly, will we all graduate?

Will you ever find out who I am?

Soon it will all become crystal clear.

See you at my party Monday night, and don't forget to bring at least *one* thing on the list. Au revoir!

You know you love me.

gossip girl